LINORE ROSE BURKARD

ONE CINDERELLA NIGHT

Copyright © 2022 by Linore Rose Burkard

Published by LILLIPUT PRESS OHIO 45068

Publishers Cataloging-in-Publication Data
Name: **Burkard, Linore Rose, author**
Title: One Cinderella Night / by Linore Rose Burkard
Description: 1st edition
Summary: A single young woman in fear for her life is forced to try and con a billionaire into paying a debt the mob is after. But can deception lead to love?

ISBN: (print) 978-1-955511-04-9
ISBN: (ebk/epub) 978-1-955511-02-5

Subjects: 1. Fiction— Christian Romantic Suspense
2. Fiction—Romance, Christian, Inspirational
3. Fiction—Romance, Billionaire, Dating, Relationships

FOR READERS WHO ARE ALSO WRITERS

Please be aware from the outset that I write in omniscient POV. That is, in 3rd person, but unlike limited 3rd person, I can move freely between characters. This allows me to write a scene more like a movie camera, capturing the inner life of more than one character in quick succession. Experience tells me that many writers of today are not up to snuff with what omniscient POV is. This is not their fault; many writing instructors are either ill-informed or biased, calling every use of omniscient POV "head-hopping." Oh, dear.

Please be advised: "Head-hopping" in its pejorative sense occurs when a reader cannot tell whose head they're supposed to be in. Head-hopping is confusing; it is omniscient POV done poorly.

My readers always know whose head they're in. You may not be accustomed to this point of view in storytelling, so consider this fair warning! Please don't leave me a bad review because you are unfamiliar with the technique.

Now that we've got that settled, enjoy the story!

Affectionately,
Linore

Bonus Alerts

"Cinderella Cakes"
Recipe
Free short story
offer

MAY, 2015 FLUSHING,
QUEENS, NEW YORK

Emma Benson fixed her lipstick and turned to her best friend Nadia Haseltine for her appraisal.

Nadia smiled. "You look great. Even Ricky's gonna wish—".

"No, he's not!" Emma's sharp tone silenced her friend. "He's not gonna wish anything except that I behave precisely as he says."

"If he doesn't tell you you're beautiful…" Her voice trailed off.

"He won't notice," Emma said flatly as she tucked the lipstick into her purse.

"He's a guy, isn't he?"

"He's a devil."

Nadia sighed. Riccardo Grasso was good-looking to a fault. Who would have thought he would turn out to be…well, like Emma said, a devil. "Anyway, you'll be a hit."

They'd spent three hours doing Emma's nails, makeup and hair. Emma had bought new white stilettoes at a bargain basement to go with the fancy dress she'd found on sale. Her slim frame made her look taller than her five-feet-five inches, and her long, dark hair against the pale dress—thanks to the deep conditioning treatment from Nadia—shone luxuriantly. Nadia was only five foot two and blonde. She was a hairstylist by trade and a powerhouse of emotional support as a friend.

Emma grabbed the present for Ricky's sister Maria that she'd agonized over, finally settling upon a loosely woven, peach-colored summer shawl. Something Maria might need on a warm summer night in Sicily, where she was soon headed. It would go well against her hair. Emma hadn't met Maria yet, but judging by Ricky's jet-black locks, she figured Maria had the same. The party tonight was in honor of her coming wedding and departure to Italy—or so Ricky said. These days, she didn't believe anything Ricky said. Why she'd even bothered to pick something nice for Maria, she wasn't sure. Maria probably wasn't even Ricky's sister. She was probably his wife! *The lying, scheming devil…*

They started up the steps from her finished-basement apartment. Nadia said, "I'm sorry, Em—I wish you didn't have to do this."

Emma locked the door behind them. "Me, too." She stopped and stared at Nadia. "I don't think I can! I know what it will take for this to work, and I can't!"

Nadia took her arm. "I know. It's horrible that he wants you to do this. But think about it. You know what's at stake!"

Emma looked tragic. "How could I forget?" They started down the walkway to the street.

Nadia shook her head. "You know, I think you should work on Ricky, soften him up. I saw how he looks at you."

"How he used to look at me."

"Still, he's got feelings. I think you could reach him."

"I don't want to reach him," said Emma. "Not anymore."

Nadia gave Emma an impulsive hug, her face scrunched in a frown. "You'll do great tonight. And pretty soon it will all be over, and he'll be out of your life forever. You can put all this behind you and get a good guy."

Emma turned distraught eyes to her friend. "Soon it will be over? Yeah, after the mob shoots me and my family in the head and dumps us in the Hudson."

"Don't say that! You're going to make this work!" Nadia's eyes filled with tears. "You have to, Em. You have to!"

Emma nodded and squeezed Nadia's hand. "I know. I'll do my best."

The young women traversed the short walkway to the pavement, stopping for traffic before crossing the street to where Nadia's boyfriend Chris sat waiting in his car.

"After you drop me off, you and Chris are going out?" Emma asked before they got in.

Nadia stopped with one hand ready to open the door. "Yeah, just dinner and a bite to eat." She gave a wry grin. "Well, for me a bite; for Chris, a huge bite."

Chris Cabrera had thick, dark hair and eyes, a meaty head and wide neck, with the body of a hefty bouncer or football player. He could look intimidating and tough but was a sweetheart. He loved online gaming but made a good income in the insurance business. Emma often wondered why he hadn't tried to play football professionally. He sure looked the part.

"You think he's gonna ask tonight?" Emma asked, studying her pretty friend.

Nadia frowned. "No way. I've concluded he's allergic to the thought of marriage."

"He just needs a good nudge." From what Emma could see, Chris adored Nadia, and Nadia adored him right back. They'd been dating for almost two years, and Nadia didn't know why he hadn't proposed yet.

Twenty minutes later, the car came to a stop before a long and stately white brick house with a porch and three Greek columns. Malba was a swanky area of Queens. Bushes trimmed to razor neatness flanked the edge of the property, while large footed urns at the entrance, filled with gorgeous greens and sprays of flowers, added to the manicured look. Neat as a pin—like Ricky, thought Emma. A long black limo sat off to one side at the curb.

Chris gave a low whistle. "These guys got all the money, don't they?"

"I'm sure most of the residents come by it respectably," Emma said, peering around at the Jewish New York neighborhood of upper-class professionals. "Doctor's Row, they call it." Ricky Grasso was assuredly not Hebraic, nor was he a doctor or engineer like his neighbors. The house and grounds, however, gave no indication he was only a high school teacher at a public school, and the limo at the curb belied it. Emma wasn't surprised because now she knew where Ricky's money came from.

"That's some limo," Chris said. He turned jovially to Emma. "Maybe you can get Ricky to take you home in it."

"I'm supposed to try and get someone else to take me home, remember?" Both faces in the front seat sobered. Emma grabbed her evening purse and the gift, stuck one leg out of the car but stopped to thank her friends. She added, "Wish me luck. Here I start my life of crime."

"No!" Nadia cried fiercely. "You are doing this to battle crime! You are doing this to make wrong things right!"

Emma's troubled eyes grew large. "But is it the right thing to do? Bringing in an innocent guy…"

"Billionaires are never innocent," Nadia said firmly. "They can't be. They're compromised, and they become megalomaniacs and want to rule the world."

"And what choice do you got?" asked Chris. "You need to do this."

Emma nodded but sighed heavily.

Nadia said, "How is Ricky gonna get a billionaire to his party, anyway?"

Emma shrugged. "No idea. I guess he'll come up with some story. More lies." She shook her head. "I can't believe I have to meet his family and pretend like we're still a thing. And that's the least of it!"

"Don't worry; you can do this!" Nadia smiled encouragingly.

"Hey—if you end up needing a ride—give us a ring," added Chris. Both friends looked back at her with sympathetic eyes.

"Thanks, you guys." Emma stepped out of the car and swallowed the lump that rose in her throat as they drove off. The lump threatened to turn into full-fledged panic. *She ought to run away right now. She couldn't do this. And it wasn't right!* The image of Adam, her younger brother, crossed her mind, and it washed away the panic.

How could she *not* do this? It wasn't only about her. Their father had died owing a hundred grand to a mob boss and now it was on Emma—according to Ricky—to pay it back. Or else.

Neither she, her younger brother Adam, nor their stepsister or stepmother had known about the debt. It was as if her father lived a secret life. But whatever he'd done, it was over; it was who he was, and nothing would change that. She raised her head and took a deep breath. Nadia was right. She could do this. She would soon have to find a different way to get out of this mess, because Ricky's plan was asking too much. But she hadn't found it yet. In the meantime, she could do tonight. Meet the guy. Keep Ricky happy. If only for Adam's sake, she had to.

Chapter Two

Peter Bentsen, the young owner and CEO of Bentsen Global Associates, took his place at the head of a long conference room table when his emergency cell beeped. It was his secretary, Kim. "I said it had to wait." His voice was terse.

"I'm sorry, sir, it's Lila, and she sounds frantic."

Peter frowned. He knew Lila was trying to reach him. They'd been going out for two months, but the meeting concerned a 760-million-dollar deal, and it was on him to make it happen. Acquiring companies—getting deals signed, making mergers happen—that's what he was good at. He hadn't become CEO of a multi-billion-dollar business by putting his personal life first.

"Tell her I'll call as soon as I'm done here."

Ninety minutes later, he tried calling but she didn't pick up. As he and Sy Goldberg, his right-hand man, headed for Peter's office, he stopped by Kim's desk. "Did Lila leave a message?"

Kim cleared her throat. "She was upset. She said she left a message on your office line because you miss the ones on your cell." Kim cleared her throat again. "And…and she said I may need to find a new job soon?" Kim's eyes were large and uncertain as she searched Peter's.

"What?" Peter gave Sy a look of incredulity. "Does she want Kim's job?"

Sy shrugged. "She came by the house this morning looking for Sofia , but Sofe's at her mother's in Massachusetts. She didn't say anything to me about Kim's job." Peter turned back to Kim. "Don't worry about it. I don't know what she's talking about, but you're not going anywhere."

Kim took a deep breath and visibly relaxed. "That's what I thought. Thank you, sir."

Peter turned to Sy. "C'mon," motioning with his head for Sy to follow him into his office. He sat down while Sy marched to the bar and helped himself to a drink. Catching Peter's eye, he motioned to his drink, though he knew it would be turned down. Peter didn't drink. The bar was for clientele.

While Peter found the message on his phone, Sy plopped a bottle of vitamin water before him, then sat a few feet away on a leather sofa. Behind them, tall windows overlooked New York City, a heady view from the 39th floor.

Peter said, "What?!" He sat there looking stunned.

Surprised, Sy asked, "What's up?"

Peter stared at his friend. "She broke up with me."

Sy's mouth hung open. Suddenly he remembered something from his encounter with her that morning. He bit his lip, thinking, then looked back at Peter guiltily. In a slow, strange tone he asked, "Did she say why?"

Peter had the cell phone to his ear, waiting for Lila to pick up. "Something crazy! She thinks I'm broke. Or our companies are broke. Something like that. I have no idea why." He met Sy's gaze with a pained expression. "How the heck could that even happen? What was she thinking?"

Sy jumped to his feet. "Wait, wait, don't talk to her! Wait a second."

"Lila—" Peter said heavily into the phone.

Sy grabbed the phone from his hand and thumbed off before Peter could stop him.

Peter jumped to his feet and lunged for the phone. "Are you crazy? She just picked up!"

Sy put the phone behind his back. With Peter coming at him, he backed up until he was at the window. "Don't talk to her yet! Listen to me. Don't talk to her. I have to tell you something." He wore a guilty expression that made Peter back off just enough for Sy to stand straight without leaning into the glass.

"What do you know about this?" Peter asked, his voice edged with anger.

"I spoke to Lila this morning," he said, his eyes large and apologetic. He shook his head. "I was kidding! It was a joke! I thought she knew!"

"What did you say to her?" Peter glared down at him, his hands on his hips.

"I told her you made a disastrous business deal and lost your money." When all Peter did was stare at him for a moment, he shrugged. "That's all."

Peter grimaced. "That's ALL? Why would you tell her that?"

Sy shrugged again. "I don't know, she's always bragging about how much money you have. You and I know you can't lose billions that are spread out in all kinds of assets in a single deal." He held his hands up. "I never dreamed she'd believe me, honest!"

Looking supremely annoyed, Peter held out his hand for his phone. Sy slowly handed it back, but he said, "You're not gonna call her, are you?"

Peter was already on it. "Yes, I'm gonna call her."

Sy grabbed the phone again and darted away. This time Peter scuffled with him and both men fell onto the sofa. Muttering under his breath, Peter finally managed to grab the phone and climbed back to his feet. Staring down at Sy he cried, "Have you lost your mind? Have you lost your freakin' mind? What is it with you? It's MY phone! I want to talk to MY girlfriend!"

Sy stared, wide-eyed, and swallowed. "Just listen, you moron!"

"This moron could fire you in a heartbeat."

Sy's lips firmed. "Listen to me. I'm your friend. She *broke up with you* because she thinks you're broke! Think about it. Do you want a woman who drops you the moment she thinks you're not rolling in dough? Is that what you want?"

Peter stared. Sy had a point. He circled the office, then paced back and forth. Hurt and anger twisted together into an ugly knot he didn't know how to release. He circled again, then stopped at the window and stared out.

At this height the skyscrapers shone with late morning sun, their windows gleaming like sheets of gold and platinum. How could he be so blind as to have missed what Lila really was?

Sy knew Peter well enough to keep his mouth shut as he watched.

Peter could understand Lila being upset by the loss, had it been real. Dating him carried certain assumptions about the lifestyle she could anticipate enjoying if they got married. But to break up with him by voicemail! She'd said, 'I'm sorry, but this is too much. You should have told me." Not even a word about how Peter would feel, must feel, at such a loss. It was all about her. In a cold wave of reality, he saw that the money meant more to her than he did. He shook his head. Fortunately, he wasn't in love. Lila was vibrantly pretty, red-headed, but spoiled.

Sy came and stood beside him. Together they stared at the city, at the people and cars far below, small as ants. They stood in silence for a full minute. Peter turned to Sy.

"We're through," he said, in a grim tone.

Sy, with a look of deep regret, watched his friend walking back to this desk. "Look, I'm sorry!" he cried. "I didn't mean to cause bad blood between you two—"

Peter turned sharply. "Not with you; I'm through with her. You're right. She was crying, but she didn't even ask me about it, didn't say she was sorry for my sake." He shook his head, his lips pursed. "I thought she was crying for me. But you know what? It wasn't about me. She was crying for the money."

Chapter Three

Lying on a beach towel on his stomach at a tropical beach with his wife Sofia by his side, Sy called Peter at his office at 12:30. The man seldom left the building to eat.

Peter swallowed a bite of sushi—his favorite lunch—and picked up. "Why aren't you here?" he asked.

"Did you forget I'm on vacation?"

"No. Um. Yes. So what's up?"

"I need a favor for an old friend. A fellow teacher from back when I was teaching."

"What does he need?" Peter continued eating.

"Well, here's the thing. He's going out with this beautiful girl, Emma. Her last name's Benson, by the way, but it's spelled differently than yours. Anyway, we like Emma."

Behind him, Sofia cried, "I *love* Emma! She's so sweet!"

"Sofe loves Emma," Sy said.

"I heard," Peter said. "So what's the problem?"

"Well, Ricky—he's the friend—he's suspicious."

"He thinks she's cheating?"

"No, not that." He smiled at Sofia over his shoulder as she rubbed a fresh coat of suntan lotion on his back. "See, he's a high school teacher, and teachers aren't usually rich. But this guy is loaded. His co-workers don't know it. His students don't know it. But he thinks his girlfriend is after it."

"After his money?"

"Yeah."

Peter huffed into the phone. "So why are you calling me?" His tone hardened. "Am I, um, the neighborhood expert in money-hungry women because of Lila?"

"Not because of Lila; because you're swimming in dough," Sy said smugly. "Well, okay, I told him what happened to you. But he doesn't want you because of that. He knows I work for you and says he can find out super quick about his girlfriend if you'll help. He thinks she's fishing for money. So he's looking for a bigger fish."

"I see where this is going. I'm not interested."

"Wait, just think about it! You were hurt by Lila. Wouldn't you want to help another guy avoid a Lila?"

Peter took a deep breath. He rubbed his temple. He wasn't exactly fuming over Lila's betrayal, but her behavior since discovering her mistake had turned him off even more.

She'd pleaded with him to take her back until he blocked her calls. Then she pestered Kim until Kim blocked her calls. She was persistent, he'd grant that.

She'd attracted him in the beginning because of that strong personality. He wanted nothing to do with her or anyone like her. "I don't have time for this."

"ONE night, Pete, that's all I'm asking. One night." He winked at Sofia, who grinned.

"Sy—" in a warning tone. "A. Don't call me Pete. B. What are you talking about? What's one night?"

"My friend—he's throwing a huge bash for his sister. It's a big family affair, the last party before she leaves for Italy."

"So?"

"So, Emma will be there. All you need to do is show up. I'll introduce you to her—"

"The fortune hunter?"

"Well—we don't think so, but Ricky says he has reasons. All you have to do is be yourself, the bigger fish."

"And let her know it." Peter sighed. "I don't know. Look, not to sound conceited or anything, but what if she just likes me more than him?"

Sy hesitated. Peter was tall, Nordic blond, blue-eyed and good-looking. "You got a point. Don't be likable. Be obnoxious."

Peter practically snorted. "Obnoxious? Really?"

"That way we'll know it's the money she's going for, if she goes for you." Slowly he added, "Just—be—rich."

"When is this party?"

"Friday night." There was silence on the line and Sy met Sofia's eyes. He shook his head as if to say it wasn't gonna work, when suddenly Peter said, "Fine. I'll do it in protest of all the Lilas in the world. Get me an invite. I'll be there. Uh, where is there?"

"In Queens, good neighborhood.

The invite will have the address. Thanks!" Sy said hurriedly, giving Sofia a smile and a thumbs up. "Leave it to me."

As he thumbed to end the call, Sofia's mouth pursed and her brows knit. "It seems unfair to Emma. She's sweet. She's …uh… authentic. I don't think she's after Ricky's money. How would she even know he has any?"

"I know, she's a good kid," Sy said. "I told Ricky he's being paranoid, but he can't get rid of the idea."

"That she somehow *divined* he's got secret millions and is after it?"

Sy rolled over on his beach towel. "I guess it has more to do with him than her. He's insecure, if you ask me."

"Because she's so pretty," Sofia said.

Sy grinned. "She's more than pretty." He looked over to meet her eyes. "Like you."

From inside the limo at the curb on Friday night, Peter watched as a car with a couple in the front seat stopped before Ricky Grasso's house. He came to attention, trying to get a look at the woman in the passenger seat in case it was this Emma person he was supposed to dazzle. He wanted it to be quick, this one night he'd promised Sy. His plan was to latch onto her as soon as possible and get the dirty work over with. He'd be polite at first. But then he'd make it clear that he had money enough to keep the most money-hungry woman alive and happy as a bear in a pool of honey.

Unfortunately, he'd have to get suggestive to see if she'd take the bait.

He wasn't comfortable about doing it, as it wasn't honest.

He'd seem like a lowlife. On the other hand, he'd be doing his duty to help another guy not fall prey as he had, to a pretty face. But he'd arrived early and still hadn't seen Sy arrive. He was supposed to make introductions or at least identify Emma for him.

While he watched, the car's back door opened. A long, shapely, high-heeled leg came out and landed on the street as its owner lingered, speaking to the others in the car. As he enjoyed the view of that one leg, he suddenly realized it could be hers. It could be Emma. He cleared his throat and got ready to leave the car. When she emerged from the backseat, he gave a low whistle. Sy wasn't kidding—a glowing brunette. Certainly could be a fortune seeker, just like Ricky thought. Why not? Any woman with that face and figure could snare a man with a fat bank account. She said her goodbyes and watched the car drive off. Her face looked strangely sorrowful.

As she took the first step toward the house, he got out of the car. He had to know if this was Emma. She glanced his way, caught him looking at her, and looked away. She hurried her pace, but Peter was closer to the entrance and long-legged. He fell in beside her. "By any chance, are you Emma?"

She froze. Two large, brown, lovely eyes surveyed him curiously. "Yes, who are you?"

"A friend of Ricky's. He asked me to look after you tonight, actually."

Emma's mind reeled. This was the guy? The ruthless billionaire she was supposed to con into giving her a settlement? So young and cute. She blinked and remembered she had to play her part. "Oh. Um, why would he do that?"

Peter hadn't prepared a why and said nothing. She looked past him at the limo. "Is that your car?" He turned and nodded, surveying the sleek black vehicle. "Yup. One of them."

"Oh…we thought it must be Ricky's." She shook her head. "I figured he rented it."

He held out a hand. "I'm sorry, I'm Peter Bentsen. I'm the CEO of Bentsen Global Associates. Hello." *How utterly pretentious. He would never normally introduce himself this way.*

"Benson?" She gave a little smile as she accepted the handshake.

"Do you know me?" His job would be that much easier if she was already aware of the family name, but then he remembered the similarity with hers.

She shook her head. "No. My name is Emma Benson."

"That's right, I was told. But we spell it differently, apparently." He took her elbow to move them on. "How do you spell yours?" When she told him, he gave the spelling of his.

"Oh, like Bentsen's Department store."

Peter smiled, his eyes sparkling. "Exactly like that." They started up the front stone steps.

She smiled, a warm, friendly smile with generous lips. "For a moment I thought we might be long-lost relatives, and since you came in a limo, I'd be the poor relation."

Peter saw an opportunity and dove in. "Well, I'm glad we're not related too," he said, staring purposely, suggestively, into her eyes.

He knew it was vulgar to leer at a woman to her face—but Sy had told him to be obnoxious. He stifled his conscience.

Emma looked away. In a voice too high she said, looking toward the house, "I've actually not been here before. Have you?"

So she wasn't ready to flirt. "You've never been here? To your boyfriend's house?"

She glanced at him. "No. He always picked me up at my apartment and we went places." They climbed the steps to the stone porch.

Peter found it curious that she'd spoken in the past tense. He *picked* me up, not he *picks* me up. And, we *went* places, not, we *go* places. Also, why hadn't he brought her to his house? But he remembered Ricky didn't want people to know about his money. The house wasn't a mansion, but he supposed it was still more than what the usual high school teacher enjoyed.

They reached the top of the steps. The front double doors, hung with heavy triple-paned glass, opened before them and two smiling faces, a young man and woman, burst out of the house. One of them partially slammed into Emma who flew backward into Peter's arms.

For precarious seconds they teetered at the edge of the top step, but he managed to absorb her weight against him without reeling backward. Gently, he moved them away from the edge, his hands about her arms.

"Scusa! Sorry!" the young man cried, looking back at them as he continued running. The youthful pair disappeared around the side of the house, holding hands and giggling.

"Thanks. That was close!" Emma said.

He nodded. "Crazy kids."

Inside, the house was cool and spacious, uncluttered and decorated tastefully in an expensive-looking mix of modern and traditional.

Sy had said Ricky didn't live like he had money, but his house was giving him away. Not so very Italian, Peter noticed. He'd expected to find a Mediterranean Old-World style, something he'd seen in the homes of many Italians.

As they followed the main corridor, sounds of gaiety ahead wafted toward them. One turn brought them into a giant kitchen/dining area, busy with uniformed caterers. The area was bright as daylight thanks to a wall of windows that overlooked the backyard, making it easy to see where the action was. They stopped for a moment to survey the scene. "Nice house," Peter murmured.

"I'll say!" Emma answered, looking around at the high-ceilinged, sparkling-clean kitchen. The presence of caterers fit right in with the expensive Corian counters, a wealth of gleaming stainless-steel appliances, and the evident beauty in the white, beveled tiles they stood on. A waiter stopped before them holding a silver tray of savory-looking hors d'oeuvres and asked if they'd like any.

"No, thank you," Emma said. Her stomach was tied in knots.

Peter took a small napkin and allowed the man to place two canapés on it before handing it to her. "Try them." He took two for himself as well. "How'd you and Ricky meet?" He took a small bite, willing her to linger there with him before joining the guests.

"He was a teacher at my high school. I wasn't in any of his classes, but we saw each other. And then one day, five years after I graduated, he started taking the same bus I take to work. His car was being repaired." She sighed.

Peter couldn't help but notice that her memory seemed anything but happy. He was surprised she didn't drive a car, but said nothing.

She continued, "After it was fixed, he started driving me to work, and then he asked me out." At the time, Emma had thought it marvelous—the handsome teacher whose company, now that she was an adult, she was free to enjoy, was enjoying her too. He was full of compliments, often calling her 'princess.' Now she knew it had nothing to do with admiration.

"So that makes you…what, 22?"

She gave a grim smile. "Just turned 23, actually."

Peter took another bite. He'd thought she was older, at least 25. At 29, he had six years on her. He felt fresh pangs of remorse. She was only a kid. But she had the air of an adult, he'd grant her that. And, young or not, if she was a fortune hunter, Ricky deserved to know.

"So how long have you been dating?"

Emma looked at Peter Bentsen curiously. He seemed alarmingly interested in her relationship with Ricky. "Just a few months," she said quietly. How she longed to tell him it was over, had been since Ricky showed his true colors. He'd been brutal about it. Emma was falling for him fast, but one day he sat her down in his car and explained that he worked for a mob boss; that her father owed big bucks to the mob. And that he'd entered Emma's life with the sole purpose of getting that money back through Peter.

"You're not eating," Peter said, motioning at her untouched appetizers.

She looked at him helplessly. "I'm a little on edge, I guess. So many new people…" She held her napkin out to him. "Here. You eat these."

Peter accepted it and took a bite of one. "What do you do?"

"I work at a hospital. Not medical," she added, hurriedly. "I'm an executive secretary."

Peter's business brain made him ask, "It is a good-paying position?"

She looked at him with the edges of her lips turned up. "Not really. But I make ends meet." She shrugged. "It pays the rent." She didn't add that the only reason it paid the rent was that her landlady was a self-proclaimed "born-again" Christian and purposely made it affordable for Emma. She didn't understand why Mrs. Akabi was so kind to her—but she wasn't complaining.

She added good-naturedly, "Until I get my degree, I'm not really eligible for good-paying jobs."

"What? An executive secretary can get a great salary—you just have to work for the right boss. Like me." He grinned. Peter forced more questions to the back of his mind, such as, what degree was she studying for? What did she hope to do after she earned it? He reminded himself he wasn't here to get to know Emma. He had to focus on what he needed to know. Was she another Lila?

Emma looked through the long windows at the guests outdoors, head bobbing as she searched for Ricky. She wanted him to see her with Peter, doing what she was supposed to. "I guess we should join the party, huh?" she asked brightly. "I'll let Ricky know we're here."

"Right." She glanced at him and her face grew serious. "What did you mean when you said Ricky asked you to look after me?" She was genuinely curious as to what lie he'd been told to get him there.

He tried to give a reassuring smile. "Exactly that. He said he'd be busy making sure everything is running smoothly and keeping his sister happy. Especially keeping his sister happy."

He scrunched his face, remembering. "Something about relatives visiting who would want his attention all night, too."

She shook her head. "Funny, he didn't bother telling me he'd hired a babysitter. I wouldn't have come." It was only half a lie. She knew she'd meet a billionaire, but she hadn't known he'd been tasked with looking out for her.

Peter grinned. "Not hired. Just doing a favor.

I'm sure he thought you'd still enjoy the night." With a wry grin he added, "I'm not half-bad, you know. You might even like me if you give me a chance."

She met his gaze evenly. "I'm sorry. I didn't mean anything against you… How do you know Ricky?"

"We have a mutual friend, Sy Goldberg."

Her eyes lit. "Oh, Sy and Sofia. They're great!" She looked out at the guests. "I hope they're here. They're probably the only people I'll know." Silently, she thought, *and the only ones I trust*.

He took her hand. "Besides me."

You gotta play hard to get at first, Ricky had said. *Don't act interested*. She gave an uncertain smile, and gently extricated her hand. "Let's go say hi." As he accompanied her outside, she said, "Remember Peter Bentsen, you're only looking out for me. I'm here because I'm Ricky's girl." Her stomach lurched at the words, but all she had to do was remember that Adam's life was on the line as well as her own. Nothing was more important than that.

Chapter Five

Emma was both relieved and concerned to meet Peter. She'd expected a middle-aged, paunchy man who was used to getting what he wanted. Someone loud, pushy, and rude. Didn't it take a long time to accrue a billion dollars? Didn't it make a man cocky and arrogant? She hadn't seen a hint of that in Peter so far. She was relieved she wouldn't be forced to spend time with the ogre of her imagination, but trepidation tempered the relief. It might be worse having to pull one over on Peter Bentsen if he was really as good as he seemed. A little too forward, perhaps. She hadn't missed that suggestive look he'd given her. But otherwise, he seemed polite and down-to-earth. She had a sudden wild hope that maybe Peter wasn't the right guy.

Maybe there were men with limos all over the place. It didn't make him a billionaire. *But Ricky asked him to look out for you. This is the guy.*

Groups of chatting guests were scattered on the property, some on the patio in plush outdoor furniture, some around a long and epic built-in pool off to the right. Others were on the lawn where white cloth-covered tables and chairs were set. To the left was a long buffet, manned by catering personnel, including what looked like a bar. One large group of guests was talking loudly in Italian, the women in vibrant, colorful dresses. *The Spanish Armada,* Emma thought. *Okay, so they're Italian, not Spanish. But they're an Armada and that's what I'm calling them.* Aloud she said, "If this is only the pre-wedding celebration, I can't imagine what the wedding will be like. Wow!"

"Isn't this to celebrate his sister's birthday?"

Emma said cautiously, "I thought it was because she's getting married and going back to Italy." Hadn't Ricky gotten his story straight? What was she supposed to say? Still searching among the guests, suddenly Emma's eyes settled on something. "There's Ricky." She made a beeline in his direction, and Peter followed.

Peter was watching her for clues as to her feelings and couldn't help noticing that she hadn't smiled upon seeing Ricky. Her eyes hadn't warmed up, either. Emma was a beautiful young woman, but it seemed that Ricky's intuition was right on the money. Pun intended.

He hadn't yet impressed her enough with his wealth. Sy's words reverberated in his mind, "Don't be likable, just rich."

But she'd never go for an obnoxious moron when she already had a wealthy boyfriend.

A bird in hand… He'd have to behave at least good enough for her to take him seriously. Get to know her a little more. Then, dazzle her. She seemed like a sincere girl, but he'd know soon enough how deep that sincerity went. And so would Ricky.

When they came up to Ricky, Peter didn't let on that the two men hadn't met before. They did the usual male quick appraisal of one another. Ricky was like a modern Dean Martin with thick dark hair and a ruddy complexion. In dress pants and a crisp shirt, he looked smart and neat. He was shorter than Peter, who was six foot two—but he could see why a woman like Emma would find the man attractive. Peter was more like a young Clint Eastwood, or so he'd been told.

Quickly he said, "Hey, Rick, nice shindig. Has Sy arrived, yet?"

Emma looked up at him startled, as no one ever called Ricky "Rick." While she continued watching curiously—a little too curiously for Peter's liking—Ricky said, ignoring the gaffe, "Just arrived. He was asking about you."

Emma took Ricky's hand. She had to play her part. "Why'd you ask this guy to look after me? I'm a big girl, you know."

Ricky smiled awkwardly, as if he believed she was being authentic. He waved an arm, "As I told Peter, I don't want you to get bored. I'm gonna be busy, and Peter's very entertaining." He looked straight at her. "You look beautiful."

"Thank you." Emma searched his eyes.

Ricky smiled and kissed her cheek.

Peter could swear she stiffened. Ricky didn't notice. But the more Peter saw of Emma, the more he suspected she didn't care for her boyfriend.

Worse—dangerously for him, he liked that. Her beauty was the kind to make a man feel good just to be around her. Lila also had that effect on men but in a different, flirty way. Where Lila emanated a sophisticated, streetwise aura, Emma was alluring but had a sweetness about her, a wholesomeness that Lila lacked. Yet it was marred by…what? Suspicion? The word "caution" came to mind, but what was she being cautious about? He'd have to keep up his guard. Emma might be more dangerous than Lila. He was suddenly enjoying the prospect of looking after her, and she seemed devoid of the calculating eyes of a gold digger, which put him at risk. He must not be fooled again.

Emma asked Ricky, "Didn't you want me to meet your family?" She had no desire to meet them, but they had to keep up appearances, didn't they? Ricky said, "Oh." He motioned to the Italian Armada. "Those are my four aunts I told you about. I'll introduce you officially later but trust me—you're not missing anything. They don't speak a word of English."

"Where are they from?" asked Peter.

"Italy. Sicily," he added as if to preclude another question.

"Riccardo!" One of the Italian Armada waved wildly at Ricky. He said, "I gotta go. Stick with Peter for now, okay? I have a lot to juggle." Above her head, the two men met eyes. Peter didn't prolong it. It wasn't a contest; they weren't vying for Emma.

And he wasn't out to prove anything. In fact, it seemed like Ricky was a first-class jerk for needing him to test his girlfriend when she was evidently not into him. Even Lila had been savvy enough to pretend she was crazy about Peter—if Emma was pretending, she wasn't doing a very good job.

Emma searched Ricky's face as if for a clue as to why he'd complimented her, saying she looked beautiful. Was he hoping to point it out for Peter's benefit? She scolded herself for wishing he'd meant it in a caring way. Why was she still attracted to the snake?

"Wait," she said, stopping Ricky from leaving. "Where should I put the gift?" She held up the box that she'd painstakingly wrapped.

"Oh, I'll put it with the other gifts," he said, taking it from her. "Thank you."

"In that case, here's mine," Peter said. He produced a small black velvet box from a pocket.

"That must be a ring," said Emma, with a little smile. "You knew her ring size?"

"It's from Tiffany's," Peter said. "She can exchange it if she needs to."

"Tiffany's!" said Ricky. "That was very generous of you." He shot a look at Emma—"I told you so," it seemed to say— and then gave Peter an appreciative look.

Peter shrugged. "No problem." To Emma he said, "Want to see it? As the woman here you can tell us if she'll like it."

Ricky handed Emma the box. She opened it gingerly and saw a sparkling diamond ring. For a moment she stared at it, trying to decide if it was real or not. "Is that a real diamond?" she asked, her voice slightly awed.

Peter exclaimed, "What kind of self-respecting billionaire would I be if it weren't?"

Emma saw her chance to appear naïve about that. She looked up at him. "You're joking, right?"

"He's not joking," Ricky said. "He's a billionaire."

"Oh. Sorry." She swallowed and looked away. *What a phony she was!*

Peter felt he was finally making progress and was glad he'd instructed Kim to pick up an expensive ring. It seemed to hit a note with Emma. Ricky, it seemed, was right about her.

When his name rang out again from the Armada, Ricky put an arm around Emma and gave her a squeeze. Nudging her forward, he propelled her in Peter's direction. "Okay, my friend," he said, smiling. "Take good care of my girl. I'll be around if you need me."

Emma watched him turn and walk toward the Italian Armada who were still speaking loudly in their native tongue. She tried to look scandalized, as if she felt awful that he was leaving her with a stranger. It wasn't easy; she was happy to be rid of Ricky and the feelings he could still evoke in her. But the injustice of the whole situation suddenly weighed upon her as if she'd been given the load of a champion weightlifter and must carry it.

She blinked back a tear. Ricky's betrayal still hurt, and now she was forced into this terrible position of having to deceive a nice guy.

Peter said, "Are you okay?"

She thought quickly. "I think he's dumping me!"

Peter took her arm and turned them around, heading toward the vibrant green lawn, meticulously landscaped with a border of exuberant spring blooms. "If he was, I think he would have told me."

She nodded but was still fighting resentment. It was so unfair to have to behave like this. She wanted to come clean, tell Peter to get as far away from her as possible.

But if she did that, nothing would be solved. Adam's face came to mind, young, studious, full of hopes for the future. He was majoring in engineering in his first year of college. The thought of harm coming to him was enough to break her heart, and worse than any fear she had for herself. *She had to see this through*.

Peter moved them toward a bright wall of daffodils.

"What did Ricky tell you?" she asked in an injured tone. She bent down to let her fingers touch the smooth yellow petals of a daffodil.

"Just what I said, to keep you company while he's occupied." He paused. "It's a tall order."

She looked up. "Am I a difficult prospect?"

He studied her. "Only because I have to behave myself and not try to steal you away from him."

She sniffed and came to her full height. "You'd think Ricky might have worried about that."

Peter smiled. "I'm glad he didn't."

Emma turned uncomfortably, gazing at the flowers again. She motioned at them. "They're beautiful."

"They're not the only beautiful thing here."

"Okay, Mr. Bentsen." She put her hands on her hips and faced him. "You're coming on awfully strong for someone trying to behave."

"Call me Peter, please." In a soft tone he added while studying her eyes, "Does it really bother you?"

She lowered her head and then looked up tentatively. "It does." It *did* bother her, only not for the reason he would think. She was trying to scam this sweet guy.

"I'm sorry. But honestly, if Ricky wanted to dump you, I'd be more than happy to take his place." He softened the words with a wry grin.

She looked away, hiding a small frown. "You don't know that. You hardly know me."

"I'm getting to know you. And Sy spoke highly of you. If Ricky doesn't swoop you back to his side as soon as possible, I'll have to admit he isn't as sharp as I thought him."

That earned him a little smile, but Emma wondered if he was for real. This was over the top, wasn't it? He must be after something every bit as much as she was. He was a typical guy, trying to score. No, he was a *billionaire* trying to score.

This was in her favor, but she had to wonder why he'd bother with a girl from Queens. Perhaps he behaved this way with every pretty girl he met. He'd said he was doing a favor for Ricky, but she hadn't seen a bit of warmth between the men. Somehow Ricky had gotten his cooperation. She wondered what he'd told Peter to get it.

He took her hand and led her to a stone bench. "Can I get you a drink? Something to eat?"

Even though Peter suspected Emma was indeed after Ricky's money, in the few moments of seeing her with him, Peter's determination to be the obnoxious rich guy had switched gears. Instead, he wanted to try the "woo the girl" mode, despite saying he'd behave. Besides, he wasn't supposed to behave. He was here to do his best to lure Emma to him, only now he really wanted to.

He hadn't felt the desire to win a woman's heart since Lila's betrayal. But Emma had visibly stiffened when Ricky touched her. That reaction served Peter an opportunity on the proverbial silver platter to start fresh with Emma as smoothly as the catering staff handing out stuffed mushrooms switched to canapés.

Chapter Six

Emma took a seat still wondering about Peter. Maybe he was just hoping to score, but he didn't have to be this nice, did he? What if he was really as nice as he seemed? What if he was a good guy? *What was she thinking? She'd never go through with this if she worried about him.*

"What would you like?" he asked. "Do you have a preference?"

"Um. No."

He smiled. "I'll get something you'll like."

She regarded him curiously as he walked off, a tall, blond, beautiful *billionaire*. The idea of having so much money was inconceivable.

To think how little her problem seemed in comparison to how much a man like that owned.

But how could he be so wealthy, so good-looking and still available? The only answer that made sense was that he must be a womanizer. He was practiced at turning on the charm, she was sure.

Emma saw now how it would play out if she followed Ricky's scheme. She'd get involved with Peter, but in the end, instead of getting a settlement, she'd get nothing. She couldn't conceive of sleeping with him—nothing frightened her more than to contemplate having sex again ever since she'd been raped ten years earlier. It was the most painful thing she'd experienced in her life. She couldn't see giving herself away for a man she loved, much less for Ricky's nefarious cause.

Sure, if she got married one day, she'd have to go through with it. She'd be in love and that would change everything. But until then, she had no intention of sleeping around with anyone. She hadn't told Ricky. He'd never tried, and if she told him when he proposed tonight's scheme, he'd have set the Mafia on her right then and there.

Despite her aversion to the thought of sex, Emma had to get a hundred thousand dollars out of Peter. She'd probably end up asking him outright, and he'd say no. Even to a man with such wealth, a hundred grand was a hundred grand. It was impossible. And it was only a matter of time until Ricky found out, and her family was dead meat.

If only there was another way. Suddenly it seemed not only hopeless but stupid. Why had Ricky come up with such a hare-brained scheme to begin with? Why had she agreed?

The questions nagged at her but the spring air was cool and lovely, and the flower-filled landscape bright and cheery.

The thought of running away from it all crossed her mind again, but Ricky would be furious, and it wouldn't accomplish a thing.

Before Peter got their drinks, he went toward the house for a quick restroom break. At the back door, he almost bumped into Ricky, who looked at him questioningly. "Going somewhere?"

"To the restroom, if you don't mind."

"Oh, of course." Ricky smiled wanly and waved him on. Peter had to admit he had a charming smile, but he didn't move. "Where is it?" Ricky's smile faltered. He motioned behind him. "Ask the help. They'll show you."

Peter didn't relish asking the help. "Just point me in the right direction."

He could swear Ricky's face blanched. "Oh, uh…" He peered inside. "That way." He pointed past the kitchen.

Peter went on, wondering why Ricky seemed uncertain, as though he didn't know the way to a restroom in his own house. Especially a house this size, which probably had at least three.

Emma, still feeling miserable, continued to consider her situation. It seemed improbable that Ricky would have a billionaire hanging around his little shindig, happy to babysit his girlfriend. Suddenly she realized that Peter must have Mafia connections too. It wasn't Sy that brought the two men into the same sphere, it was the mob!

She broke into a light sweat. *Wait. I'm catastrophizing. I always imagine the worst.* If Peter was in the mob, then he would know that she didn't have the money to pay the debt. What would he gain by coming on to her? Ricky had already done that very successfully. Gotten close just to put a noose about her neck. She knew from Sofia that Sy did indeed work for a billionaire—it had to be true that he was the connection. Sy and Sofia Goldberg were funny and warm. Maybe she could ask them for help. But what if Sy was in on the scheme? He'd go straight to Ricky if she complained or sought help.

"Emma!"

She looked up and was surprised to see Sy and Sofia coming toward her. Sofia, a dark brunette with Mediterranean-olive skin, stood a good three inches taller than Sy, who was no Romeo in appearance. But they were one of the happiest couples Emma had ever met. Sofia waved madly and smiled. A pang of guilt twanged through Emma. Surely the couple was innocent. Ricky had told her his job as a teacher was his "alternate life." It was how he became friends with Sy, who was a former science teacher before climbing the corporate ladder. To other teachers and everyone at the school, Mr. Riccardo Grasso was just a typical high school teacher, an all-around good guy. No one knew his connections to the Mafia cartel that had Emma by the throat. And he'd warned her that it had to stay that way.

He'd introduced her to the Goldbergs, a friendly, gregarious couple, on double dates. They were generous, inviting Emma twice to their house on Eaton's Neck, Long Island, "Millionaire's Row," as they called it. She'd been impressed by the ritzy and tasteful estate, coupled with their down-to-earth easy manners. They didn't have a shred of snobbishness.

She stood to exchange kisses on the cheek with them.

"What, did Ricky leave you alone?" Sy asked.

"I'm waiting for Peter—." She was about to explain who Peter was, belatedly remembering that Sy knew him already.

He said, "Good. I didn't see him yet. But I saw his limo."

Sofia leaned in and said, "How do you like him?"

Emma sighed. "He seems nice. We just met." She looked at her curiously and said, in a defeated tone, "He's the guy Sy works for?"

Sofia chuckled. "Don't be so down about it. He is. He's Sy's boss! And I think he'll give Ricky Grasso competition tonight." She leaned in again. "Competition he needs if you ask me."

"He needs more than that," Emma said sourly.

Sofia's eyes widened. "I may tell Peter you said that."

"Oh, please, don't."

She snorted. "Ricky was stupid to bring him in!" With a mischievous grin she added, "But Peter ought to know he has a good chance with you. All's fair, remember!"

So Sofia knew about this strange situation. Emma bit her lip—she needed to know what else Sofia knew. She took her arm and walked a few steps away from Sy. "Can you explain why a billionaire—your husband's boss, no less—is supposed to keep me occupied while my boyfriend ignores me?" If Sy and Sofia weren't in on Ricky's devious plan, surely they would find this curious.

Sofia opened her mouth as if to answer but they both realized that Sy had kept pace and was listening. Sofia turned to her husband, her brows high. "Yes, dear, can you tell Emma why that is?" Her lips were pressed together. She turned to Emma. "Good question!"

Sy didn't blink. "I invited him. Ricky asked if I knew anyone who could keep a beautiful woman company tonight. Knowing his relatives would keep him busy, he felt bad for you."

"I said I would keep you company!" Sofia interjected. Sy acknowledged that with a nod but added, "He didn't want you to feel like a third wheel. He said to find a guy." He studied Emma and then leaned in toward her and Sofia . "I suggested an ugly guy, but he said no, find someone good-looking."

Sofia nudged her husband in the arm. "Tell her the rest!"

Sy looked regretful. "Okay. Peter's a great guy. Religious, too. But just between you and me—he put a hand near his mouth and whispered. "He's on the rebound from a broken heart."

Sofia stared at Sy with brows raised. Sardonically she said, "A broken heart?"

Sy continued, "So while he thinks he's taking care of you, be kind to him. He needs a good woman."

Sofia slapped him on the arm and cried, "That is the worst possible thing you could tell her! You know what it will look like to Peter!"

Emma's eyes sparkled with amusement, but she was also confused. "Why is that the worst thing he could tell me? Because of Ricky?" The Goldbergs, it seemed, were truly in the dark about Ricky's mobster ties.

Sofia nodded at Emma with large eyes. "Yes, because of Ricky. He's testing you!"

Sy took Sofia's arm and said, "That's enough. We told her enough."

Emma understood. Ricky told the Goldbergs he wanted to test her loyalty by pushing her toward a great-looking guy. And he knew Sy worked for a handsome billionaire.

How sly he was. She said, "I still can't believe that Sy's boss has nothing better to do on the weekend than attend this little shebang in Queens."

Sy winked. "All I had to tell him was that you're beautiful."

Emma smiled, but suspected the couple knew more than they were revealing. She kept the conversation going, hoping to nudge more out of them. "I would have been happy hanging out with you and Sofie."

Sofie clucked her tongue. "You see? Why didn't we take care of her?"

Sy made a dismissive sound. "Now you can say you spent the night with a billionaire."

Emma gasped. "I would never say that. You know what that sounds like, don't you?"

Sofia gave Sy a nudge with her elbow. "Emma's a good girl, remember? She'd never spend the night with a guy just because he's loaded."

"Oh, right. Sorry."

"What are you sorry for?" It was Peter's voice. He handed Emma a tall glass topped with whipped cream and a cherry, with a straw. Still speaking to Sy he said, "Did you insult my date?"

Emma had raised the straw to take a sip but lowered it quickly. "We're not on a *date*." She gave him a reproving look.

"Wishful thinking." He smiled.

She shook her head, but there was a smile at the edges of her mouth.

Sofia took her elbow and said, "C'mon, let's sit. They're going to talk shop."

"How do you know?"

Sofia smiled. She had very thick, dark brows. Emma thought that on the wrong face, they'd be overbearing, almost unsightly. But on Sofia's strong features and Roman nose, they were perfectly attractive. "Because they can't be in the same room together and not talk shop."

"What do they do?" Emma asked.

Sofia looked at the two men and nodded her head. "They pull strings. They run lives."

To Emma's questioning look, she smiled and added, "They buy up small businesses and make them big. They do mergers, and acquisitions, and… I don't know what else." She gave Emma a big grin. "It pays the bills."

Emma wanted to know more. "What is your husband's title?"

Sofia's face scrunched in thought. "He's technically Vice President of Marketing." She smiled again and said, "There's six of them, but Sy is Peter's right-hand man. He used to work for Peter's father and watched Peter grow up. They go back a long way together."

When Emma only nodded soberly, she looked at her with concern. "Hey, I know you must feel hurt by Ricky."

Hearing the words brought a lump to Emma's throat. Sofia didn't know the half of it. She thought Emma was hurt by being fobbed off onto Peter, but if that was it, Emma would dance for joy. She wished she'd never met Ricky, with his secret life in the mob. He was a "collector," he said, and Emma's father died owing them big. The revelation about her dad coupled with Ricky's deceit were two of the biggest shocks of her life. But she couldn't think about Ricky and the phony he was, or the way he'd hurt her, now. The hurt from his betrayal was fading, but the terrible burden of her father's debt and what she must do to pay it back was weighing her down. Ricky had destroyed her world, but said he had a plan. A way for her to make it right. All she had to do was cooperate and do her part. This night was the start of doing her part.

Such thoughts must have made her appear crestfallen. Sofia continued, "Think of it this way. It could be worse. He could have said, 'Don't come.' Or he could have said, 'I'll be right with you,' and left you alone. Instead, you have Peter Bentsen. How many girls get such a guy to watch out for them at a party?" She smiled.

Emma met her eyes. "It doesn't seem fair to him."

"What?" Sofia's thick brows furrowed. "Why?"

Emma shook her head. She could not say, "Because I don't want to con him." So she changed the subject. "I feel like he's not a normal human being. I have nothing in common with someone so wealthy."

Sofia looked bemused. She nodded understandingly.
But she said, "You have a few things in common, you know."

To Emma's questioning look, she said, "Us, for one thing."

Emma touched her arm. "Thank you. I know you're trying to make me feel better." She hesitated. "If Ricky and I break up—I hope I'll see you again."

Sofia looked troubled, but said confidentially, "I like Peter better, anyway. He's trustworthy." She held a finger to her lips. "Shh. Don't say I said so." She added in a matter-of-fact tone, "Ricky said nothing about wanting to break up with you. Let him have this night with his relatives. It's a big deal for an Italian family. He'll come back to his senses when it's over."

Emma nodded, her face still pensive. Sofie's eyes filled with concern. "Look," she said, checking to see that the men were still occupied.

"I'm not supposed to tell you this."

"Yes?" Emma's heart quickened. Was Sofie going to admit awareness of Ricky's scheme?

"Ricky's insecure. He wanted a rich guy to look after you to see if you'd be interested in someone else—a bigger fish, you know?" She looked earnestly at Emma, her large olive eyes filled with sympathy. "It was a creepy thing to do. I told Sy it wasn't fair to you." Her face brightened. "But you know what? If you and Peter hit it off, you should go with it. Take the bigger fish." She shrugged and smiled. "Why not, right? Peter's a doll. And we'll still be friends!"

Emma forced a smile. Sofia said, "Ricky might think you just went for the money, but hey," she smiled at Emma. "You can live with that." She paused and added, "Ricky's more suspicious than I ever took him for."

Emma nodded. "It takes time to get to know Ricky."

Now it made sense. Emma could be sure the Goldbergs had no idea of Ricky's real goals. He had them fooled about who he was and what this night was really about. Just as fooled as she had been while they dated. She could trust them. Suddenly Emma wanted to tell her everything. "Sofe—"

"Yes?" Her friend smiled kindly at her.

"Emma!" Ricky stood over them, looking warningly at Emma.

Sofie exclaimed, "There you are. Watch out, Ricky, I told Emma to go for the bigger fish if she gets the chance. You set this up; you'll only have yourself to blame if she does." She smiled widely.

"I know, I know," Ricky said, taking Emma's arm. "I just need to tell her something." He pulled Emma along and spoke tersely into her ear. "The Goldbergs know nothing. If you tell them, I will know—and you can kiss your brother goodbye. He goes first."

Chapter Seven

Emma blinked back tears at Ricky's words, but the anger that rose in her throat she could not hold back. "Why are you doing this?" she cried.

"Lower your voice!" he hissed. He looked at the others and smiled.

"Why do you live this way?" She asked, in a lower voice. "Working for them?"

He froze, his face working with emotion.

Peter and Sy were suddenly there, both of whom joked lightheartedly with Ricky about his squadron of relatives, two of whom could be seen pointing at him and waving animatedly. Peter's height next to Sy was more pronounced a contrast than Sofia's. Ricky nodded, hardly acknowledging the men, gave

Emma a final warning look that she understood as sinister—
and hurried off.

"I don't think that man is enjoying his party," said Peter,
looking after him.

Sy said, "Sofe, honey, we need to say hello to Jim and
his wife over there," he motioned with his head across the
grounds. "He's another old friend from my teaching days."

Sofia nodded. "Okay." She turned to Emma and winked.
"I'll see you later." As she and Emma exchanged a quick peck
on the cheek, she whispered in her ear. "And don't worry
about Peter. He grew up rich and he's used to it, but he's not a
snob. I really like him much better than Ricky. I don't think he'll
compromise your standards."

Emma thanked her, happy to hear Peter was no snob, and
ridiculously relieved that he might not compromise her standards,
which she took to mean he wouldn't insist upon a bedroom scene.
Sofia wouldn't have said that if she hadn't meant it.

As soon as they'd gone, Peter said, "Why don't we sit and
enjoy our drinks?" When they were seated, he said, "How's
yours? You like it?"

Emma realized she hadn't tasted it. "I forgot about it."

"While it's in your hand?"

She gave a wan smile. "I was talking with Sofie." She
obediently took a sip. She'd expected something alcoholic, but
it tasted like sparkling fruit juice. "Non-alcoholic?" she asked.

He nodded. "Do you mind? I don't drink much myself."

"No, this is perfect." *At least he wasn't trying to get her
drunk.*

"Sofie's great, right?" he asked.

"Yes. I love her. I hope, if—" And there she stopped.

She didn't want to say anything about her and Ricky not dating in the future. They certainly wouldn't be. But he'd been her tie to the Goldbergs, and she wanted to keep their friendship.

"You hope?" he prodded.

She sighed. "I was just gonna say, I hope I don't lose their friendship, even if…."

"Aah," he said, eyeing her sagely. "Even if you and Ricky don't last?"

"Right."

"Well, lucky for you, I happen to be good friends with the Goldbergs, too." He winked at her.

"Yes, that changes everything!" she quipped. "But you're not just friends; you're his boss."

"You *were* talking to Sofie!" He took her hand. "Let's move." He led her back to the cabana housing the buffet, and they joined the line. He took her drink and gave it to a caterer. "We'll get another after we eat." He handed her a plate, napkin, fork and knife, while she smiled because he was being so solicitous. Motioning her to precede him, they started down the first table.

After they chose what they wanted and found a seat, Ricky came by as they ate. Emma put her fork down and eyed him cautiously. Did he want to issue another dire warning? Remind her that her brother's life was in her hands? Or, was he going to introduce her to his family to keep up the charade? It would be a natural thing to do if they were dating. But all he did was ask about the food, was it good, did they enjoy the caviar, and so on. He met Emma's eyes. "You okay?" he asked. "Is Peter taking good care of you?" He looked at her searchingly.

She knew the real questions behind his words. *Are you doing what I told you to do? Are you getting him hooked?*

"He's great," she said in all seriousness but without enthusiasm. And he was—he'd been solicitous of her all along, quick to get her anything she wanted, quick to inquire, and never put out by it. Ricky nodded. "That's good." Looking at Peter, he said, "Thank you, man."

"No problem." Peter eyed him dispassionately.

Ricky turned back to Emma. "I'm sorry about tonight."

Her eyes shot up to his. He wasn't sorry. Was he sorry that she was being forced to live a lie because of the sins of her father? Was he sorry that Peter was merely a pawn in his plan? In his eyes she saw the usual hardness she'd learned to recognize since he'd let down his mask. But he was playing the game and expected her to play along. She said, "I know it's a special family occasion."

He nodded approvingly. "Right." He leaned down and gave her a quick kiss on the mouth. Emma again stiffened involuntarily.

"Gotta go. I'll see you later." He strode off, heading back to the passel of relations who made up the Armada, the only people at the party who seemed to matter to Ricky. Emma saw a young, dark-haired Italian woman with them, talking and smiling. Maria, no doubt.

Peter turned to her. "Got room for dessert?"

Emma smiled. "I don't eat much sugar, but I did see a yummy-looking trifle. They're not too sweet. Maybe a small helping." She went to stand but he touched her arm. "Allow me. A gentleman should always serve a lady." And with a little smile, he was off.

She'd never known another gentleman, it seemed, because she couldn't remember ever having a man serve her on a date.

She sat there wondering if he was for real or just being extra nice. But she had to admit, it felt nice. The heck with feminism if it meant you couldn't accept a little chivalry when it came your way. There was far too little of it in the world anyway.

When he returned with two small dishes of the trifle and handed her one, she smiled. "You like trifles, too, in small amounts."

He sat down and took a spoon of the whipped cream. "I agree with you about sweetness. A little goes a long way." He raised a brow. "Look at that. We have something in common."

She nodded, smiling inwardly at his choice of words. It was exactly what she had complained about to Sofia, that she had nothing in common with a man like Peter. But this helped explain his slim good looks. He no doubt worked out, too—probably at his own private gym in his house.

After they'd eaten, he said, "You like flowers. Let's walk around the grounds."

Tall fences circling the area were lined with wide flower beds, all meticulously landscaped with dark mulch and sharp, clean edges. The colorful array of spring blooms was truly gorgeous, a mini botanical garden. And not just tulips and daffodils, though there were plenty of them, but multi-colored pansies and bright, small blooms that Emma couldn't identify. In one corner stood an ornamental cherry tree, its lush pink blossoms looking as feminine and bedecked as a bride.

When they left the stone patio to approach the perimeter beds, her stilettoes sank into thick grass and she had to grasp Peter's arm to steady herself. Peter stopped walking and put a hand upon hers on his arm. Glancing at her shoes, he said, "Maybe you should take them off."

She looked down, considering it. "My feet will pick up grass." Looking up again, she smiled. "But—why not?"

Holding onto him with one hand, she bent to peel off the shoes. To her surprise, when she finished, he bent down and undid the laces of his, and then removed them, as well as his socks. When he stood up again, he said, "I couldn't let you be the only one barefoot."

Her eyes glittered. "Thank you." Slowly they traversed the grounds, sharing admiration for the blooms. When they returned to the starting point, they each put their shoes back on, but first Emma held up one of hers, surveying the soiled heel.

"Darn," she said. "And I just bought these."

"Oh?" Peter seemed interested. "Where do you get your shoes?"

She straightened up and searched his eyes. Was he going to judge her for buying cheap shoes? Probably. He would no doubt buy the ritziest brands, probably foreign.

"Why do you ask?"

He smiled. "Our first family business was retail, still is." Before she could ask for more details, the young couple that had knocked into them earlier came running past, the young boy chasing the girl again. Emma moved closer to Peter to get out of the way. The young lady decided Emma and Peter made a proper barrier for her to circle, and did so, giggling, while the boy followed in pursuit.

"Hang tight," Peter said, his lips turned in a smile.

When they'd circled three times, they finally ran off.

Emma said, glancing at her feet, "I'm gonna run inside; I need to wipe off my heels." He stayed with her as she crossed the stone patio, went past the Italian Armada and food cabana, and started up a set of stone steps. A sharp crack sounded, and she lost her footing. She would have fallen backward if not for Peter, who caught her solidly in his arms.

"My heel snapped!" she cried. "I can't believe it. I'm so sorry. So much for new shoes."

He smiled roguishly, looking down at her still in his arms. "Good thing I was here to catch you." He winked. "I seem to be coming in handy for that tonight."

Emma blushed, for it was absurdly true. He'd caught or steadied her earlier on the front porch, once on the grass, and now again. She'd only known him for a little more than two hours. Staring into his very blue, very pleasant eyes, she said only, "I need to go home."

Chapter Eight

Peter helped her to her feet. The broken shoe was caught between two stone steps. He eased it out. Emma blushed furiously. Not only for losing a heel at a posh party but for almost falling—and both in sight of the Italian Armada watching from the patio. Were they talking faster and more excitedly than ever?

She took off her other shoe—better than limping unevenly. Peter gave her a sympathetic look as they proceeded to the house to retrace the path to the front. She stopped to look around for Ricky before going in and did so again as they walked through, but there was no sign of him.

Well, that was that. She couldn't worry any more tonight about Ricky's plan, because she couldn't go on with one shoe.

Maybe heaven was giving her the "out" she needed. She'd gone to church for the first time in a year to pray for help. Ricky would have to come up with some other scheme. She felt regret about leaving Peter, though she was glad that she wouldn't have to try and con him anymore. He seemed a delight. Then she remembered that he was probably an experienced womanizer.

She turned to him. "Thank you, Peter Bentsen, for sticking with me tonight. It was…" she hesitated. "A bad night—"

He winced.

"But it would have been a lot worse without you," she finished hurriedly. "I'm calling for my ride," she said, opening her purse for her cell phone.

He touched her hand to stop her. Cocking his head to one side he said, "It's not even dark yet. The night's still young. I'd like some more of it to change it for you, so you won't think back to it as bad."

"Thank you, but I've got a broken shoe and a bruised ego and I'm ready to call it a night."

He nodded but said, "In that case, let me take you home." He led her to the front portico and motioned toward the limo.

She hesitated, but a little smile curved her lips as she looked at the shiny sleek vehicle. "You'll take me home in that?"

"Of course."

She looked up at him. Should she accept the offer? Would he think she owed him something for his trouble? Sofia had emphasized that Peter was a good guy. She liked him better than Ricky. Emma said, "If you promise you aren't going to try anything."

He raised his brows.

"Miss Benson, you injure me!" he said in a mock offended tone. "Then, with a wry grin said, "I won't try anything my mother wouldn't approve of."

Emma smiled but shook her head. "I don't know your mother, so that doesn't help."

He grinned. "She's a good woman, but okay, I won't try anything that you don't approve of."

Emma smiled. "Deal."

Seated in the plush leather interior, Emma had to admire how having money had its perks. Peter pressed a button and said, "Bentsen's."

"Bentsen's? I hope you mean the department store and not your home."

He smiled. "The store."

"Why? You said you'd take me home. You haven't even asked for my address."

"First things first," he said. "I promise to get you home safe and sound. But we must do something about those shoes, first."

"What? What do you mean?"

He didn't answer but took one of the shoes from her hands. He peered inside it to read any inscriptions.

Then he looked it over, handling the shoe like a shoemaker, feeling the top and assessing the sole. She took a deep breath, telling herself it didn't matter what he thought about her bargain shoes.

People like Peter didn't live in the real world. She'd done the best she could with what she had. It turned out that the best was junk in this case, but how was she to know that beforehand?

He put the shoe down. "Hey, check this out," he said. He took a pair of headphones from a compartment tucked into the door and put them over her head. Instantly, soothing music hit her ears. She smiled. Andrea Bocelli! She loved Bocelli. They had another thing in common.

Peter drew a cell phone from his suit jacket and made a call. Emma decided she was not supposed to hear the call—hence the headphones—so she tried to relax and enjoy the music. It didn't surprise her in the least that he'd mix business with pleasure. Didn't over-achievers always do that? And if a billionaire wasn't an over-achiever, who was?

Soon they pulled up outside the nearest Bentsen's Department Store. She'd seldom been inside, as the swanky store prices were above her pay grade. Occasionally, if she did go in, she'd move like a magnet to the clearance racks.

While they sat there, Peter continued to talk into the phone. At one point, he picked up her abandoned shoe again and looked it over while speaking. Finally, he put the phone away. Emma removed the headphones.

"That was great. You like Bocelli too?"

He nodded. "I do. Now we have two things in common."

"I guess we do." A reluctant smile curved her lips. She looked past Peter at the store entrance, since they were parked right in front of it.He'd made no move to get out, and that was fine with her. The very idea of going shopping with him in tow was unnerving. No matter what she chose, he'd probably think it tacky. She'd end up spending far too much, more than she could afford, as a result. "So…can I go home now?"

"Home? Not yet!" He turned and looked at the entrance.

"I'm sorry, I really don't want to shop. I am not worried about replacing my shoes, honestly. I have other pairs."

He turned back with a little smile. "You have other shoes? Honestly?"

"Don't make fun of me. I just don't want to shop."

He studied her a minute. "Sorry. But most women like to shop."

"I do…just not… now."

"Why not?"

She hesitated. "I don't feel like shopping, and I would never feel like shopping with someone I hardly know, anyway."

"That's it?"

"That's enough."

Peter studied her. He seemed to be thinking hard while he looked at her, as if she was an enigma he had to solve. He leaned toward her. In a confidential tone, he said, "What if I told you that you could go in there and buy anything you want? Anything. You could buy a whole wardrobe. I'll pay."

She stared at him, then let out a breath. "I'd say you had an ulterior motive, and I can guess what that is."

"And you'd be wrong. I said I would keep my distance. No strings attached. You could go in there right now and buy anything your pretty little heart desires."

Emma took a deep breath. She gave Peter a troubled look. "I'm ready."

His eyes lit with a strange light. "To shop?"

"To go home. Thanks, anyway. That was an offer I'll always remember…" she said, sardonically.

His eyes narrowed, but he studied her again. "Why?"

"Why what? Why won't I take you up on an insane offer?"

"You know I can afford it."

She shook her head. "I don't—I don't see what that has to do with it. I mean, okay, it wouldn't break the bank for you, but the why question here should be directed at you, not me. Why would you want to buy me anything, much less a whole wardrobe? That is just…crazy weird. I would like to go home, please."

Peter shifted on his seat to face her fully. "What's difficult to understand? Maybe I'm trying to win you over."

She frowned. "That's not how you win someone."

He licked his lips. "In my experience, it doesn't hurt."

She looked past him through the window and saw two store clerks carrying packages approaching the limo. Peter opened his door and they handed them in. After putting them, one by one, on the floor, he handed each clerk a bill. Emma could only guess what it was—a twenty? Fifty? "Thank you, Mr. Bentsen!" they cried, both wide-eyed and breathless, before turning around. Sharing an excited giggle, they headed back to the store.

Peter turned to Emma. Giving her a mysterious look, he picked up a package, opened the bag and drew out a shoe box. He opened the box and pulled out a pair of classy white and gold pumps. They weren't stilettos—the heel was about one and a quarter inches. He held one in his hand like a shoe salesman and then fell to one knee on the floor in front of Emma. He went for her foot.

"May I?" he asked.

Emma was dazed with the realization that he'd ordered shoes for her. ORDERED them by phone and had door-to-door service.

But why should it surprise her? Money was power, isn't that how the saying went? They'd even known his name—and then it hit her. There was no coincidence here. Peter had said his family's first business was retail. How dense could she be? His family owned the store. Offering her carte blanche for shopping was something he probably did with all his women. Or maybe he was just testing her, trying to determine if she was a fortune hunter. The worst thing about that was—it was true! Not usually, but tonight it was true.

She was in need of a fortune and purposely hiding it, though not exactly hoping to get it from him. That she considered a futile effort unless she'd compromise on her limits—and she wasn't ready to do that.

He waited for her permission to slip the shoe on her foot. It was gorgeous, must have cost a great deal, she was sure. But she said, "I don't want your shoes."

He puffed out a breath. "They're not mine. I bought them for you. It was my fault you broke your heel."

She gave him a doubtful look. "Your fault? No. They were lousy, cheap shoes, you know it."

"Please—accept them. You don't have to like me or want to see me again. There is nothing I require from you in return." He paused. "Take it as a gesture—of friendship."

"You want to be friends?"

"I'd like that."

They eyed each other. Peter's eyes were honest, not effusive, nor suggestive. He held out a hand. "C'mon, shake my hand."

She hesitated but did, sheepishly. If only she really could be a friend. A friend would tell him everything, tell him that

Ricky was hoping he'd want more from Emma, and be willing to pay generously for it. He took her heel and gently slipped her foot inside the shoe. He took out the second shoe and did the same for her other foot.

"How do they feel?"

"They feel good," Emma said, pressing her feet into the carpeted floor of the limo.

"You have to walk on them to know, really." He opened the car door and hopped out, extending a hand to help her do the same.

When she held back, he said, "C'mon, take a few steps."

But she shook her head. "I'm sorry. It doesn't feel right."

He got back in the limo. "They don't fit?"

"No, they're great. I just feel uncomfortable accepting them."

Peter paused, studying her. "Have I offended you?"

She said nothing.

"Emma. Are you offended?"

She frowned at him. "By the shoes? No. But if you think I can be bought—or bribed—like I'm for sale, you're wrong."

He bit his lip. It gave him a little dimple on that side of his face. But his being attractive was just annoying. She wasn't allowed to have a real relationship with him—not even a real friendship. Friends were honest with each other.

"I guess…" he said slowly, "you could say I was hoping you were."

It was precisely what she expected from a mega-rich guy.

He sighed. "You're a beautiful woman. You know that. But… you're a delight. I didn't expect to enjoy this party, but because of you, I did. I could have taken a lot more of you…a whole lot more." His serious, matter-of-fact tone would have been soothing if his words weren't appalling.

She took a deep breath. "I know exactly what you're insinuating."

"I'm—no! I'm sorry! I only mean it was too short."

Here was her chance. She could give him a little encouragement. She could say, "Well, we can see each other again if you like." Or something like that. If they didn't see each other again, her brother was a goner!

"Please—" she began. She was going to burst if she didn't say something and suddenly it occurred to her that she could point blank ask this man to loan her the money. How many men on earth could you ask to loan you a hundred grand? Not many, but he was one of them and heaven had put him in her path. If he loaned her the money, all on the up and up, she wouldn't have to deceive him about anything. She could pay off her father's debt and keep her brother safe and be done with the whole business. She was ready to explode if she didn't ask him. But a terrible thought prevented her. *What if he says no?* If he did, she'd blown her chance, and all hope was lost. Banks wouldn't loan her more than ten thousand dollars—she'd tried that. Ricky took it as interest on the debt. He said it would buy her time, keep her safe for maybe two to three weeks. Two to three weeks!

No, Peter Bentsen was her biggest hope, but she mustn't rush things. She'd have to ask at the right time. This was not it.

"Please," she said again.

"Take you home?"

Emma struggled for what to say. Despite the hopelessness of Ricky's scheme ever working, she had to ensure that she'd see him again.

When she didn't answer, he picked up an intercom and spoke into it. "Let's go, Jack." He turned to her. "150th Street, right?"

She nodded. But then turned to him and felt a cold shudder. This whole experience since she stepped out of Chris's car and met Peter, had been weird. Now it felt macabre. She'd never mentioned where she lived.

As the car pulled away from the storefront and turned toward the exit to the street, she swallowed and said, "How did you know where I live? I never mentioned it." For some insane reason, she felt hurt as well as alarmed. She hoped it didn't show in her eyes.

His lips pressed together. "It's not a bad reason, not what you seem to think."

"So how did you know?"

"I think Sy told me."

She eyed him uncertainly. "Why would he tell you that? Why would you ask?"

"I don't know. I don't remember how it came up. It was in passing, I guess."

She saw earnestness in his eyes, but something more. Something that worried her. She felt sure there was a missing piece about this, something strange going on. But what? Thinking back to Sy and Sofia, she knew their attitude toward Peter was not suspicious. She thought back to Sofia's words about him: trustworthy. Ha! She'd trust Peter Bentsen as far as she could throw her broken shoe. But why would Sofia have misled her? Suddenly she didn't know what to think.

Peter said, "Since I only have you for a few more minutes, may I ask you something?"

Emma nodded. "Okay."

"If you could go anywhere in the whole wide world, where would it be?"

She eyed him dispassionately, her lips pursed. He had seemed really nice earlier, but was he about to proposition her? "I am not going to answer that. You'll say, 'Oh, well, I can take you there.'" She dropped her voice to mimic his. "For as long as you like. I'll pay."

Peter smiled. "You're absolutely right. I'd say that. Look, I happen to have a luxury yacht that's better than a five-star hotel. Why don't you come with me for a weekend? Or a week? We can relax and enjoy getting to know each other. We can take all the time in the world."

She gave him an aggravated look. This was exactly what Ricky wanted her to do, but the idea made her sick. If she went, she'd likely get that settlement. But she knew what he wanted. She couldn't do it. "Just stop. I want to go home. Now."

He leaned toward her again. "I'll make it very worth your while."

She was ready to cry. He was offering exactly what she ought to be jumping at, and despite all the danger to herself and her family, she would turn it down. She was too afraid. She was a fool! This was the opportunity she needed! He'd no doubt let her set the price, and it would solve all her troubles! But with a sinking heart, she knew she couldn't do it. She could never do it. She couldn't sell herself. Aside from her fear, it was morally wrong, and the very thought filled her with repulsion.

She said, "You'll make it worth my while? By making me a—a slut?"

"No, no, I'll hire you as my secretary and pay ten times whatever you make now."

"Leave me alone."

"Are you afraid of water?"

"No!"

"Then what is it? Why won't you jump at the chance for a dream job and a free vacation? And I'll be there to shower you with attention."

She bit her lip. "If you don't know what's wrong with that offer, well; I'm not telling you."

He looked unmoved. "O.K. There must be something you would want. Jewelry?"

She said nothing, just pursed her lips. He'd seemed so nice! Now he was nothing but a predator.

"There must be something you would go for. Some way to.."

She raised her brows. "To what?"

"To make you leave Ricky. To make you mine."

She stared at him and her lips pursed harder. "It's all about winning for you, isn't it? Beat the other guy. Win the girl." She looked away. How much she would love to tell him that Ricky wanted him to win her. That he was behaving exactly as that evil-minded minion would have him do! That would knock his pride down a notch or two.

She said, "I really thought you were a nice guy. I'm glad you showed your real colors. But I have asked you nicely, three times, to please take me home. If you don't make this car move, then you are holding me against my will. Another name for that is kidnapping."

Peter stifled a grin.

Emma couldn't believe how Sy and Sofie were completely wrong about Peter Bentsen! He was not a good guy, not trustworthy, and had thoroughly bad morals!

But now he looked at her with eyes full and earnest. "I'm sorry. I've been horrible, I know. I'd love to start over."

"Too late. I know you too well for that." She reached down and removed the new shoes.

"No. You don't know me at all!" He looked at her earnestly.

"Really. I would never normally suggest any of those things to a woman, much less one I've just met."

She glanced at him sourly. "Sure."

"No, I mean it. Look—why don't we start over—will you have dinner with me sometime?"

"No." There was no hesitation, no need to think about it. There wasn't an ounce of her that wanted to see him again. But Adam's face came to mind and tears popped into her eyes.

Peter's face scrunched in concern. "Hey, are you…are you *crying?*" He moved toward her, so she moved further away and turned to hide her face. She wiped off a tear and scolded herself. She'd put herself into an impossible situation by agreeing to follow Ricky's plan.

She ought to have gone to the police, or no, the FBI, despite Ricky warning her not to. He'd said that if she did, the mob would know, and her family would end up at the bottom of the Hudson. She thought of Adam, blissfully unaware of their father's transgressions. If the FBI entered the picture, they'd have to find him at school and pop the bubble of bliss he lived in. They'd have to do it before the Mafia got to him. And what if they failed?

Peter blew out a breath. "I'm sorry for what happened earlier, those offers I made. I really am." He turned in his seat to face her. With very earnest eyes he said, "I had to do that, you see? I have to know…about a girl…before I risk anything."

Emma's brows wrinkled. "What do you need to know?"

He swallowed. "Whether she's in the market for the highest bidder. Whether she can be bought."

Emma's mind spun. She thought she'd ruined her chance to get help from Peter, but had she accepted his offer, he would have retracted it anyway! When she said nothing, he added,

"I've been burned. Some women are only out for what they can get, especially from a guy like me. They want stuff, perks. I needed to know if that was you."

She turned to him. "So you were testing me."

He frowned. "The more you resisted, the more I wanted to know. So I kept raising the stakes. I'm truly sorry. But I've learned the hard way, I have to do that."

Her heart felt lighter. "Well, I can understand that. A man in your position." Now it made sense, why Peter could be so sweet and fun at the party and then become so abhorrent. She gave him a smile. "I'm glad you told me that. Now I can still like the Peter I met earlier."

He smiled back. "Good! Because I like you. Now, will you have dinner with me sometime?"

Emma looked troubled. "I would like to." She took a deep breath and spurted out, "The truth is, Ricky and I have been on the rocks for weeks."

"I wondered."

"Did you?"

"Something was missing between you two. Does he know you feel that way?"

"I'm not sure. " *Oh, he knows, all right! If only she could tell Peter. If only she could tell him all of it!* But he'd just tested her to see if she was after his money, and she'd passed the test. She could not reveal to him now that she did indeed need a hundred grand! Or that she was exactly what he was trying to avoid. A woman who wanted to get something from him.

"Want to talk about it?"

Emma leaned her head back against the plush upholstery, closed her eyes and sighed. "You would never believe me or understand, even if I try to tell you."

Peter's eyes sparkled. "Whoa, that's mysterious! I love a mystery." He smiled. "Try me."

Emma frowned. "I can't." She sat up suddenly and faced him with large, earnest eyes.

If she hadn't been obviously upset, Peter would have smiled at how pretty she looked.

The limo pulled up in front of her apartment building. She looked past him and said, "Wait. How did you really know my address?"

Their eyes met and she saw there was something in his that went deep. "What aren't you telling me?" she said, softly. "What was tonight really about?"

He hesitated. "If you'll have dinner with me tomorrow night—just this once—I'll explain it to you. Everything I know."

"Explain it now."

"I want to see you again."

She looked away, thinking.

He said, "Are you engaged? Has he proposed?"

"No, he hasn't."

"But if he did, you'd marry him? The guy who ignored you all night?"

A flash of hurt in her eyes made him almost sorry for what he'd said. But if Peter could learn in a few hours that this girl was no fortune-hunter, why didn't Ricky know that by now? "How long have you been dating?"

Emma paused. It felt like a lifetime ago when she hadn't known Ricky, but it wasn't that long at all. "Only about five weeks."

Well, Ricky was an idiot, Peter thought. Five weeks or five

months, the man should know by now that Emma wasn't to be bought. The fact that Peter had dated Lila for months without realizing she was a fortune hunter, didn't deter his opinion.

Behind them, a car honked. He grabbed the intercom. "Go around the block."

Emma's face scrunched in concern as she turned to watch her building disappear from view but going around the block wouldn't take long. She could handle it.

She cast troubled eyes on him. "Please tell me what this was all about. Why did you come to Ricky's tonight? I don't think you two are really friends."

He nodded. "You're very…intuitive."

"Yes?"

"But that's all I can say, I'm sorry."

She sighed. "Fine. I'll get it out of Ricky."

His lips pursed. "If you have dinner with me tomorrow, I'll tell you what he probably won't."

Was there really something else going on that she didn't know about? Alarm filled her breast. "Like what?"

A stoic look. "I'll tell you tomorrow." He paused and then said, "Even if you speak to Ricky, how will you know if he tells you everything until you hear what I have to tell you?"

This seemed to hit the mark. She nodded. "OK."

They'd rounded the block, and the limo came smoothly to a stop. Peter checked traffic for a moment, then jumped out of the car and came around to Emma's side to hold the door for her. "I'll walk you to your apartment."

"You don't have to. I'm right down the hallway."

"I want to," he returned, with a smile.

Peter had a sweet smile, a boyish one. It belied his being a powerful executive, and Sy's boss.

At the door to her apartment, he said, "You weren't kidding. You're right on the first floor."

"This door goes downstairs actually, right to my apartment."

She drew out her keys, her thoughts in a jumble. Peter seemed like the sweet guy she'd met at the party again, but was this the real Peter, or was he really the man who propositioned her? Was he really testing her? Why wouldn't a powerful man be manipulative? Used to getting what he wanted? What if he was just playing her, inferring that something was going on, simply to get her guard down? But why? He could have any number of beautiful women.

She unlocked the door, then turned back to him. She let out a breath. "OK. So, tomorrow night. How should I dress?"

"Fancy. Like you are tonight."

"You think I have a closet full of fancy dresses?"

His eyes clouded. "Don't worry about it. Wear what you're comfortable in."

She nodded. "Okay." Looking at him curiously she asked, "Are you sure you don't want to tell me more now? It'll save you a dinner bill." She grinned.

"I can't wait to talk more with you. Tomorrow night." He pulled a slim case from an inside shirt pocket and drew out a business card. "This has my office number—for the future." He turned it over, drew a pen from the same pocket, and wrote on it. "And this is my cell. Call me if you need anything." He handed it to her, then leaned in and kissed the side of her face. "It's been a pleasure. I'll pick you up at seven tomorrow."

Chapter Nine

At around 11 pm that night, Ricky called Emma. "You left early. Why didn't you let me know?"

Emma wished she hadn't answered the call. "I left with Peter—I figured you'd be pleased. And I did look around for you. I didn't know where you were."

"Did he ask you to leave with him?"

"I left because my shoe broke. He insisted on taking me home." She wasn't going to give him all the details. Certainly not about how she'd rebuffed his advances. He'd have her head.

"You should have had someone find me."

Sardonically she said, "So you could give us your blessing? It was better I didn't."

Ricky fell silent. Then he asked, "Are you with him?"

"Who, Peter?"

"Who else?"

"Of course not." She paused. "But don't worry—I'm going out with him tomorrow night."

Ricky exclaimed, *"Perfetto*! That's a good princess."

"Don't call me that!" He used to call her princess in an affectionate way and Emma had loved it, but now it made her angry.

"So, what's your take on Bentsen? Think you'll manage him?"

"Unless he's putting me on, he's sweet. I think I can just ask him for a loan."

"No, no, no!" Ricky's tone was sharp. "Don't do that. He'll want to know why you need it and he's very savvy. You won't get away with lying about it. And if you tell him the truth, the family will find out and you'll be sunk."

"Why? What do they care how I get it as long as I get their money?"

"Look," he said. Emma could picture that smooth Italian face looking so fine but hiding a devil. "There's trouble right now. They don't want attention."

"Killing us won't be getting attention?"

"Are you kidding? These are professionals. You and your family will disappear without a trace. They're smart. Don't push them, Emma."

When she was silent, he added, "And don't say a word. If you tell Bentsen, you make him a target. No amount of money can protect him from these guys forever. If he knows, he's dead, *comprendonio?* You don't need a loan. You don't want a loan. He'd be crazy to give you one in the first place; you couldn't repay him in a hundred years. You need a settlement. You want a settlement. Play your cards right and Bentsen will give it to you."

"What if he doesn't?" Since she had no intention of cooperating in the manner Ricky wanted her to, this was a very real possibility.

"*Dai,* Emma, he will! Or you know what will happen!"

She had nothing more to say. Ricky was obviously married to the scheme, no matter how tenuous and uncertain it seemed to her.

All that night, Emma tossed and turned on it but could not escape the nagging feeling that if she didn't come clean to Peter, he'd somehow get wise to her anyway, and then it would be worse for her. Only she couldn't come clean!

And doing it Ricky's way wasn't an option because she wouldn't sleep with Peter to get a settlement. She'd tried not to think about it, tried to believe that when the time came, she'd do whatever it took. But after last night's propositions, she realized she wasn't for sale, period.

She ought to be, with what was at stake. It seemed downright immoral of her not to be, but now she knew that her determination not to be used again was stronger than reason, stronger even than her need to protect Adam. Her stepmother and stepsister were in danger too, according to Ricky, but she definitely couldn't give herself away for them. What had happened to Emma ten years ago was her stepmother's fault, to begin with.

She thought of confiding in Sofia—maybe she and Sy could get a loan out of Peter. But they would have to know why; and she'd be putting them in danger, just as Peter would be in danger if she told him.

She called Peter's cell at 10:30 a.m., not wanting to risk waking him if she called earlier in case he slept in on a Saturday.

"Emma! I'm glad you called. I was just about to call you."

"How'd you know it was me?"

"Please tell me you're not backing out of having dinner with me tonight."

"I'm not."

"Great! How are you? Do you need something?"

Now that you mention it, I could use a hundred thousand bucks. All she said was, "Do I need to be fancy tonight or not? I have enough time to get a dress if I need to."

"You don't need to."

"You sure?"

"Very."

"Do you want to tell me where you're taking me?"

"Sure. The Rainbow Room. A friend of mine is giving a private dinner, but I told him I'd need a quiet table for two and he said no problem."

"Oh, okay." Emma had no idea where or what the Rainbow Room was, but she wasn't about to advertise her ignorance. "So…dress for a party."

"Yup. I'll pick you up at seven. But don't get off the call yet."

She smiled into the phone. "See you at seven."

"Wait—I'll bring your shoes."

"Oh! Well, okay, thanks." That was awkward, but it did save her the trouble of buying new shoes. Just then, her doorbell rang. "I have to go, someone's at the door."

"Take the phone with you. Go answer it."

"You want to stay on?"

Peter, in his penthouse, glanced at the time. "I certainly do."

Emma was surprised, but she started up the stairs, phone in hand. "Do you have something else to tell me?"

"Yes," he said, expansively. "I hope you like it."

"Like what?" She opened the door to find a delivery man with a large shopping bag that said, "Bentsen's" in large, swirly letters.

She gasped. "Peter! What is this?"

"Are you Emma Benson?" the man asked.

"I am."

He held out a pad with a pen attached. "Please sign here, ma'am."

Emma signed and he handed her the bag with a smile. "Compliments of Mr. Bentsen."

She thanked him and shut the door, shaking her head. "What did you do, Peter? What did you get for me?"

He said, "Open it up and you'll see."

Downstairs, she put the phone on the sofa while she gingerly drew out an evening gown from an abundance of pretty tissue paper. Holding it up, she caught her breath. It was beautiful, golden, floor-length and sequined from top to bottom.

Surprisingly light in her hands, it had short sleeves and a square-cut bodice and looked to be close fitting.

She grabbed the phone. "Peter, it's gorgeous! But you shouldn't have! This is embarrassing."

"Not at all! It's my pleasure. Did you try it on?"

"Not yet."

"Try it. Send me a pic."

"I will not." With one hand, Emma held up the dress in front of her before a mirror.

"Okay, I'll have to wait until tonight. But let me know immediately if it doesn't fit right, or if you don't like it."

She checked the label. "It's my size," she said. "I already love it.

It's beautiful!"

"Good."

"How did you know my size?"

"I, um, I'm just good with that. I'll tell you more later."

"Okay." She paused. "Thank you, Peter. I'm amazed that you did this! But no more gifts, okay? If I didn't need this for tonight, I wouldn't accept it."

"Gotcha."

She was still admiring it, running her free hand over the swanky fabric. "Well, I hope I wouldn't," she said, wondering if she'd really turn down such a beautiful thing.

Peter chuckled. "I'll see you later. Oh—check the bag again."

Before she had a chance to, Peter ended the call. She checked the bag, and sure enough, down in all that tissue, there was a long white slip—perfect for the dress.

How sweet and thoughtful of Peter to send her a dress and a slip! On the other hand, how did he know her size? Mixed feelings swept through her. The idea that he was a hopeless womanizer seemed like the only answer. He was so used to women—and their clothing—that he had correctly guessed her size! She shook her head. What was she getting into?

But first things first. She removed the tags from the slip and put it on. The price tag for the gown made her stop in shock. It read, $664.00! She felt almost afraid to wear it. The suspicion that Peter was still trying to buy her crossed her mind. But she slipped it over her head and stood before a long mirror. It was a mermaid cut to the knees, then flared out just enough to drape softly against her legs.

She pulled it gingerly to fit just right and couldn't believe how flattering it was for her figure. Of course. Peter had perfect taste. Her phone beeped and she went for it, thinking it would be Peter texting to check that the dress fit. It was Nadia.

"I'm outside. Let me in," she texted.

Emma hurried upstairs to open the front door to the building. Nadia's eyes bulged when she saw her, and then smiling, she exclaimed, "Wow. Wow. Wow! Where are you going?"

"C'mon in," Emma said, pulling her inside. "I'll tell you about it."

"You bet you will. How did it go last night? The least you could have done was answer my texts."

"Did you text? I missed it!" Emma cried. "Sorry. Anyway, now we can talk. Did something happen with Chris?"

"Of course not. He's never going to propose. If I want to get married, I'll have to ask him." She looked admiringly over Emma's gown. "When did you buy that dress? I never saw it on you before."

"It's new. Shut up and listen..."

After Emma filled Nadia in on the previous night's events and how Peter had sent her the dress and a slip, Nadia sat down, looking rapt. "It's love!" she said, looking at Emma like she was Joan of Arc. "It's love! He's falling for you!"

"No, he's rich, and very good with women," Emma corrected. "He knows how to turn on the charm. And how do you think he knew my size? He's got so much experience that he can tell a woman's size by looking. Doesn't that give you the creeps?"

Nadia looked doubtful. "Em, can't you ever believe for the best? You know, you always put a negative spin on everything."

"Maybe, but you always put a positive spin on things. *'It's love!'*" She mimicked.

Nadia made a dismissive sound. "I'd rather be me with my positive spins than you with your negative ones."

"So would I," Emma said, honestly. "But you're not positive about Chris proposing. And it's not my spin threatening to murder me and my family. This world is negative, and that's that."

Nadia sighed and peered into the Bentsen's bag still sitting open on the sofa while Emma went through her stockings to make sure she had a pair without a run.

"Great! It's not my spin telling me I don't even have a decent pair of stockings to wear tonight. Want to come with me to get a pair?"

When Nadia was quiet, Emma looked over at her. She was holding up an unopened pair of expensive stockings, grinning from ear to ear. "Boy, this Peter thinks of everything. Look at these! $39 bucks! They look like silk! You gotta keep him, Em."

Emma frowned. "I gotta get a hundred thousand from him, you mean." She put her head in her hands. "I can't stand it! I can't even stand having to say that! He does seem like a really sweet guy—it scares me. He makes me just want to get to know him and not have to think about needing anything! It's so unfair!"

Nadia came and put her arms around Emma. She stroked her hair. "I know, it is. It is." When she pulled away, she said, "Are you sure you can't go to the police or something? Maybe they can get you out of this."

"They'll find out. Ricky said they would. He said they've got moles everywhere. If I tell, we're dead. He even said if I tell Peter, that'll put a target on him too."

Nadia blinked at her. "You told me. I don't have a target on me."

"I hope not!" cried Emma.

Nadia sat back down. Soberly she said, "Me, too." But she seemed to shake the worry right off. Nadia had a way of doing that. Popping up from where she sat, she said brightly, "Let's do something special with your hair."

Emma wished she could be more like her optimistic friend and shake off worries like that. It would probably never happen. But she smiled. "You're the hairdresser. Whatever you say." They entered Emma's surprisingly large walk-in closet where she took off her gown and hung it up carefully while Nadia dragged a chair in front of the mirror. She spotted the price tag on the gown and grabbed it. "Oh. My. Gosh!" She stared at Emma incredulously, and then her eyes lit up.

"I got an idea," she said. "I saw it in a magazine. You have the right hair for it." She clucked her tongue. "We can't have you looking the same as last night."

"Horrors! We can't have that," Emma echoed playfully.

"Em," Nadia said, coming from behind her to face her. "Some men really notice hair. This Peter guy seems like the type who would." She looked at Emma as if she'd just given her the facts of life and there was no arguing with that.

"You're right. He does."

They moved a floor lamp for better lighting and Emma looked up the Rainbow Room on her phone while Nadia called Chris to tell him to bring her box of salon supplies. Most of her stuff was at the salon where she owned her own booth, but some she kept separate so she could do the occasional job outside the shop. Chris had a key to her apartment.

"Oh, my gosh," Emma said, staring at her phone. "This Rainbow Room is gorgeous! Look at the view."

Nadia came beside her and looked. "Wow. Good thing he sent you that dress. You're gonna need it."

"I know. And look—it's only available for private parties. And no prices listed—you know what that means."

"Uh huh," Nadia's head bobbed in agreement. "Big bucks."

While they waited for Chris, Nadia washed Emma's hair in the sink, covering it loosely with a towel afterward.

"You're not cutting it, right?" Emma asked. "I wasn't prepared to cut it."

"I just want it shiny clean," Nadia said. She ran up to let Chris in when the bell sounded, spoke to him for a minute, and then appeared back downstairs with her supplies in their pastel pink carrying case. "Okay. Let's do this. Want some music?"

"I got it," Emma said, thumbing her phone to her preferred music app. In a few moments, the soundtrack to a song from"Phantom of the Opera" began.

"I love this," Nadia said.

Before long, both women were singing at the top of their lungs with Emmy Rossum. Nadia slapped some gel into a palm, rubbed her hands, and then spread it through Emma's damp hair. She used a blow dryer until Emma's long brown hair was almost dry. Parting the hair, she fashioned the locks into a tight French braid but stopped halfway, leaving a good amount unbraided. She wound the remainder into a chignon and pinned it up. As Emma watched her hair taking shape, she thought about the coming evening and seeing Peter again. She was surprised at how much she looked forward to it. Despite the ever-present weight hanging over her head, and the discomfort because she couldn't be honest with Peter, she looked forward to seeing him, and yes, to wearing the gown with her hair freshly done.

Nadia had kept an inch of hair on the sides of Emma's face from the braid, which she now used a curling iron to coax into sweet, coiled tendrils. "Rainbow room, here we come! You look great with your hair up," she added, circling Emma to make sure every hair was in place.

"Because you are great with hair," Emma replied, smiling.

"I'm great with great hair. Yours is thick and holds a curl, and you haven't ruined it with perms or blow drying."

"Well, I think you're great with hair, period. And I love this look. Thank you!"

Nadia gave a pleased little smile, her eyes still on the task, adding a final pin to Emma's chignon. "What are best friends for?" She grinned. "Now. Let's do your makeup and pick the right jewelry."

Chapter Ten

Peter was anxious to see Emma again. Ricky hadn't intended that to happen, but all was fair in love and war, right? His only regret was if Ricky knew Emma was seeing him again, he'd think she was the fortune hunter he believed her to be, that she'd gone for the bigger fish. Peter knew without a doubt how untrue that was. He didn't want Ricky to get the wrong idea, but Emma said their relationship was on the rocks anyway. Whatever happened between Peter and Emma, it was the man's fault for doubting Emma and bringing them together.

When the bell buzzed—it was so loud it always made her jump—Emma nervously went to open the door. Peter stood there looking immaculately handsome in a gorgeous white tuxedo, including a white vest and tie. He'd looked handsome last night in a dark suit, but this was handsome on another level. Expensive tailored clothing certainly went far on a man. His blonde hair and blue eyes against all that white looked downright angelic. She eyed him up and down quickly and smiled. "Wow. Look at you." She motioned for him to follow her, missing the look of delight that lit his eyes. "I just have to grab my purse."

From behind her, he said, "You deserve a 'wow' yourself. You look beautiful."

She turned to thank him with a little smile. He held up the pair of pumps she'd left with him last night.

"And put on my shoes," she added, smiling. "Thank you." She motioned for him to descend the stairs ahead of her, but when she joined him below on the carpet, he turned from surveying the place and looked her over again. "Don't mind me," he said. "But I knew that dress would suit you!"

"Yes, good call," she agreed airily. She decided not to mention that it was undoubtedly his experience with women that gave him such a particular talent for dressing them.

"You really look beautiful," he added.

"This dress would make any woman look great," she said.

"Oh, no. The dress doesn't make the woman, the woman makes the dress." Emma gave a little smile in lieu of an answer because she didn't have one. Peter looked around.

"You've got an attractive studio here. Glad to see you have a window—even a door to the back. Is there a yard?"

Emma nodded. "A small one," she said, moving to take the shoes from him, but he wouldn't release them. "Hold on a sec," he said. He went to peek out the window beside the back door, but the view was blocked by a cement staircase that led up to ground level. He looked at her interestedly. "Is the yard exclusively yours?"

"My landlady lives upstairs, Mrs. Akbari. It's her yard, but I can use it whenever I want. And she has permission to come through when she wants it. But she hardly ever does."

He nodded. Walking around, she heard him murmuring. "Fully finished…, kitchenette, living area, nice sofa and two recliners…, desk, chair and plenty of books"—he stopped and looked at her. "Because you're a college student." Emma nodded in amusement. He added, looking back at the stuffed shelves, "And you love to read."

His eyes landed on her easel and a painting in progress. "And you paint!" He moved to get a better look at the watercolor, a landscape, and nodded. "And you're good at it!"

"I'd be better if I had more time for it."

"You're good already. Do you have more?"

She went and pulled out some of her art, choosing a few of her best to show him. She chose a few pen and ink sketches, another watercolor, and a pencil portrait of Nadia. She loved spending time on art and was getting better and better due to her classes. In an ideal world, she could make a living at it, but that was a pipedream.

As if reading her mind, Peter said, "You could do this professionally. You're really good."

"You think so?" She grinned. "I only showed you my best work."

"But this is what you're capable of. With time and effort, all your work can be this good." Emma beamed on the inside. He turned to continue his "inspection," much to her amusement. Good thing she kept the place neat and clean. He perused her bookshelves. Afterward, he glanced at the corner with her bed and nightstand and came back toward the small dinette area adjacent to the kitchen. He pointed at a closed door. "May I?"

Emma nodded, grinning.

He smiled. "Sorry. I'm always interested in apartments—we have a real estate business. Rentals are a big piece of that pie." He opened the door and saw her bike and other stuff. "Wow. Good size closet. But where do you keep your clothes?"

Emma showed him her other closet, a walk-in with plenty of space and a long mirror on one wall. She was thrilled when she first saw it. Lots of apartments and even many homes didn't offer such a roomy option. It was where she got dressed, did her makeup and where Nadia did her hair. The chair was still there, along with various pins, a hairbrush and hair spray.

She explained that the last door past the kitchen led to a storage area with a washer and dryer. The storage space was for Mrs. Akbari, but Emma was allowed to do her laundry there.

He faced her. "It's a great little place, especially for a basement."

"Liar." She grinned. "This must look exactly like what you think all of Queens is. Dinky and serviceable."

He raised a brow. "No, no. Queens has some great areas. Lots of money here." He paused. "This is nice. I mean it." His eyes strayed to her feet.

"Let's get those shoes on!" He went for the sofa and Emma followed. He patted a spot for her to sit. When she did, he fell to one knee before her and Emma realized he was going to help put on the shoes as he'd done in the car. "You don't have to help me," she protested, reaching for the shoes.

He pulled them away. "I do. Or I can't tell if they fit right."

"I'll let you know," she murmured, but he had already lifted one of her feet by the heel. He cradled it in his hand a moment, then eased the shoe on with the smooth aplomb of a shoe salesman. He did the same with the other one, pressing on the toe of each shoe afterward to judge the fit. His comfort with doing so made her wonder just how many women he'd done it for. He was no novice, that was certain.

"Do they feel good?" He was still on one knee, his face level with hers. Emma couldn't help but notice how very blue and penetrating his gaze was.

"Yes."

"Stand and walk a bit and then see." He took her hand and helped her to her feet. "If they don't feel exactly right, I have two other sizes in the car, one bigger, one smaller."

This made Emma stare. "Peter, the traveling shoe salesman."

He laughed good-naturedly. "Right?

Emma walked across the room to try out the shoes. She remembered now that the store clerks had brought two large shopping bags to the limo last night. Now she knew what was in that second bag—more shoes in case this pair didn't fit! Who else but the rich would do that?

Peter was leaning against the divider between the kitchen and living area. He noticed a few stamped envelopes and couldn't help seeing that at least the top two were for charities. One, for a homeless shelter, the other for a women's pregnancy center. He glanced approvingly at Emma.

"They feel great," she reported, looking down at her feet. "Like I'm walking on a cloud!"

"Walk over here," Peter said, moving into the compact kitchen area. "Carpet softens the feel of a shoe. You know to always try a shoe on solid flooring before buying it, right?"

"Umm…no, I didn't know that."

"Now you know. Stores put good carpeting on the shoe area to make shoes feel better." "Walk over here," he said, moving to the kitchenette.

He watched her circling the small area. "How do they feel?"

"Wonderful." She looked down at her feet. "Even with heels. They still feel great." They were pretty and cushioned—usually pretty didn't come with comfort. Usually, she had to choose one or the other—at least at her pay grade. She looked up. "They're perfect, Peter. But I'd like to pay for these, at least. I don't want to wear a complete outfit that you bought."

He gave her a patient look. "Now, now, let's not get petty. They're a gift." He walked to her. Emma wanted to argue but felt the absurdity of it. He was a billionaire, for goodness' sake. "Well, I shouldn't let you buy them for me—or the dress—but thank you. They look and feel great."

He took her hands and gently forced her into a spin as if they were dancing. He met her eyes, her hands still in his. "And you look great." Emma searched his deep blue eyes and saw nothing she did not like.

Peter cleared his throat and checked an expensive-looking smartwatch. "Shall we go? Traffic's probably heavy on a Saturday night."

She got her purse and they started for the stairs. Peter motioned with an arm for her to precede him. "Ladies first," he said, smiling.

Emma walked past him acutely conscious of his presence behind her, a tall, great-looking guy with a smile that was beginning to melt her heart. At the top of the stairs, she remembered she'd meant to wear her faux fur shoulder wrap that would go perfectly with the dress. She'd never had an opportunity to wear it before, and since it was early May, not too warm for it. She turned to tell him she had to get it, but, because he was two steps lower, she found herself face-to-face with him.

Then, to her horror, instead of saying she forgot her wrap, she heard herself impulsively blurt, "You look really good, too!"

You look really good—what was she, a teenager?

Peter grinned. "Thank you very much." He seemed ready to move on, so she said, "I forgot my wrap. I have to get it."

"Oh, tell me where, I'll get it."

Emma went to move past him. "No, it's okay, I'll get it." And promptly she slipped and would have fallen had he not caught her in his arms.

Looking into her eyes, he said softly, "We seem to be making a habit of this."

"I'm sorry." Emma felt her face getting hot.

"No problem." He smiled, then hovered his lips over hers. Without kissing her, abruptly he straightened—and hit his head on the ceiling above the steps. "Ow!

"I'm so sorry!" she cried again. He rubbed his head. "No problem." His voice was heavier than before. He helped her get steady on her feet. "Tell me where it is," he said again.

Emma wouldn't dare risk tripping again on the narrow stairs to get it herself. "In my closet—on the right."

He bounded down the steps and was back in a minute with the wrap. When they were outside the door, Emma locked it. He put the wrap about her shoulders. "Very pretty," he said. She thanked him but as they went to the walkway, she was still kicking herself for saying, *You look really good.* Like a twelve-year-old. What else could she have said? You look handsome? That would have worked but sounded old-fashioned. You look sexy? She'd never say *that*—though it was true.

Outside, sitting conspicuously at the curb was a long white limousine. Not the sleek black model from the night before, but a sparkling white, incredibly long (it seemed to her) limo worthy of a Hollywood red carpet. A uniformed chauffeur stood at the ready, waiting to open the door.

She turned to him. "Isn't this over the top?"

He took in a deep, relaxing breath. "It is; but I thought I should match my tux. And your shoes." He smiled.

"It's so huge! What have you got in there, an RV?"

"Something like that." He took her elbow and helped her enter the opened door. When they were both comfortably seated in the spacious white leather interior—sort of like a mini living room—Emma tried not to gape at the luxury surrounding her. The car rolled away from the curb. She cast a perplexed look at Peter.

"Yes?"

"I, um, looked up the Rainbow Room. I hope I don't embarrass you by being gauche or anything. I'm not used to rubbing shoulders with upper crust people in that kind of place."

His brows rose. "What kind of place do you think it is?"

"Super swanky. I'm just an ordinary girl. I have nothing in common with or you or the people who will be there."

His lips pursed. "I don't agree. I'm proud to have you on my arm. And we have more in common than not."

She looked around. "Until last night, I was never even in a limousine before."

He inched closer. "That is unfortunate. I think you deserve the best."

"You don't know me enough to say that yet."

"I'm glad you said, 'yet.'" Peter smiled.

Emma glanced out the window and saw they were heading down Northern Blvd. toward the Van Wyck Expressway. She had to admit it was a little exciting to be going into Manhattan in a stretch limo with Peter, much less to one of its more exclusive venues.

"I saw on the website that there's dancing after dinner?"

He gave her a bright look. "I'm looking forward to it."

She swallowed. "I don't really know how to slow dance."

"That's okay, I'll lead you."

"You'll have to."

"No problem. You'll appreciate those shoes on the dance floor."

"I already appreciate them," she returned, smiling. As the car wound its way through traffic, she remembered how comfortable Peter seemed when it came to shoes. "How do you know so much about shoes?"

"I used to be a shoe salesman."

"You?" Her brows rose.

He smiled. "My father is a big work-ethic guy. We've always had money, but he wasn't going to let his son grow up without knowing the value of work. He wanted me to earn my way. So in my teens I worked for two years in the shoe department."

She smiled. It made him more human, more understandable. "You must have worked in a high-end shoe store. You know about the best brands."

"Oh, yeah. I worked in the family store." He paused. "Well, it used to be all ours; we still own the majority share, but we have stockholders. Anyway, when I was younger, it was our store, but don't think that made it easy for me. As I said, my dad believes in earning one's way. I was treated no better than any other employee."

"Did you help women try on shoes?" She figured he'd been a stock boy but could not resist asking.

"Of course. Hundreds."

Emma bit her lip. Here she'd been thinking he was a womanizer when his ease with shoes and fittings was due to simple hard work.

"So have you held other jobs?" she asked.

He smirked. "Before shoes? Let's see. I cut lawns, I delivered newspapers, I even drove a taxi for a short while."

She let out a breath of a laugh. "That's a surprise!"

They turned west onto Queens Boulevard but then braked sharply. Stopped mid-turn in traffic, pedestrians swarmed past the car as they crossed the street, many talking as they did so, but no sounds hit her ears. She realized the car was soundproof.

Peter continued, "The taxi thing was my idea. I guess I thought there was some excitement in it. But my father didn't like it. I quit after two weeks." He paused. "After shoes, I managed women's clothing in our store in the Hamptons for about a year."

She felt a rush of guilt. So that's why he knew about sizes! Nadia was right that she jumped to negative conclusions about things.

He gave her a searching look. "Ok, enough about me. Tell me about your work, and how you got started."

At that moment she noticed the glittering Manhattan skyline, coming into view as they crested a rise, with the 59th Street Bridge ahead of them. She looked admiringly at the beautiful, twinkling lights, seemingly so peaceful. Behind those lights was a world of humanity with all its angst and suffering, victories, and defeats. But from here, it looked appealing and promising. She didn't get to see this often and it always made her feel like Dorothy seeing Oz for the first time.

Peter, watching her, smiled. "The route's shorter through the tunnel, but I seldom take it just so I can see this. I never get tired of it." He pressed a button. Overhead, a panel slid away and suddenly the night sky was there, stars blinking down benignly. Peter said, "I thought you'd enjoy the view. This is why I came for you so late. I wanted the sun to be down."

He got to his feet on the leather upholstery and held out a hand to Emma. She removed her shoes with the slim heels first, and then let him help her up. He put a protective arm about her when she came to her feet and stood beside him. Heads out of the sunroof, wind streamed over their faces. Nadia's handiwork of careful curls whipped across Emma's eyes and face. It was exhilarating.

He turned to her with a grin. "I should warn you," he said, speaking loudly so the wind didn't zip away his words. "I'm just a big kid with a grown-up job. I love to do this!"

She smiled. Ahead, the skyline loomed with glittering clarity, beckoning like a welcoming committee. She reeled a little with the movement of the car and Peter tightened his arm around her. As the city got closer, its fairy quality remained, and she glanced at him in star-struck wonder, smiling broadly. "It's gorgeous, isn't it!"

He smiled, nodding. "Wait until you see the view at dinner."

They crossed the bridge and made a right onto East 60th Street, then a left onto 5th Avenue, but she and Peter remained at their perch. Emma loved the close-up views of the ritzy shops and throngs of people as the limo moved slowly along with traffic. It surprised her that most people paid little attention to the gleaming white limo, or to their heads popping out of the top. When traffic got heavier, slowing to stops and starts, he squeezed her shoulder, and they sat down. The ceiling panel slid shut and she put her shoes on.

"Thank you, that was great!"

He nodded, suddenly recalling a time when Lila had refused to stick her head out because it would ruin her hair. As if reading his thoughts, Emma said, patting her head, "I must be a mess! Nadia would kill me if she knew."

"Why?" he asked, as he made a mock show of examining her hair, even taking her chin in one hand to look at each side of her head. He gently patted a wayward tuft into place. "Your hair's great. And you've got a great profile. Who's Nadia?"

"My best friend. She's a stylist. She did my hair."

He made an approving, "Mmm. She did good."

They turned right on W. 49th St., and then right again onto the Avenue of the Americas. Emma couldn't help but keep tabs on their whereabouts. She didn't get into Manhattan often. But between gawking out the window, she explained how she'd worked as the receptionist in doctor's offices since she was fifteen, before going full-time at the hospital.

"A receptionist at fifteen?" He raised a brow and nodded approvingly. "Not bad!"

"I worked my tail off," she said, smiling. "The first office I worked in was for an internist who specialized in cardiology. I did the phones, scheduling, filing, escorted patients into exam rooms, did EKGs, spun bloodwork for labs, developed chest X-rays, collected fees, filled out insurance forms—you name it."

"Wait—you did ALL those things?"

"And billing. And tidying up. It was cheap slave labor for a cheap doctor. But I was young, and I didn't know any better."

His eyes creased sympathetically.

She went on to explain that after working for a surgeon, she was hired in a small private hospital, and from there moved on to a bigger and busier one.

"What about family?" he asked. "How long have you lived alone?"

"I have a little brother Adam who I adore, a stepmother and a stepsister. Adam lives on campus at Cornell University—he won a scholarship! But believe me, the "steps" were happy when I moved out. Five years ago."

Peter did a quick calculation. His brows furrowed. "So young. What made you leave at eighteen?"

She sighed. "My dad died. They never cared for me to begin with, but it got worse after he was gone.

From the day my dad remarried, no—from the day they moved in with us, I no longer felt welcome in my own home. They wouldn't include me in anything they did, I wasn't allowed to borrow anything without them freaking out, and I had to do all the menial cleaning jobs. I hate to say it this way, but really, I was like Cinderella!"

Peter's lips firmed. "I'm sorry." An unbidden thought came: if Emma was Cinderella, and if their relationship deepened, he'd be her Prince Charming! And she needed one. No matter what they spoke about, Emma had an air of sadness that seemed just below the surface. He'd love to erase that sadness. Time would tell.

"What'd your dad see in your stepmother?" he asked.

Emma paused. She pictured her stepmother Loreen, all five-feet-four of her, in one of her cute tennis outfits with a visor, blonde hair in a thick ponytail, and her ever-ready fake smile. Her stepsister with burnished red hair was also very attractive, painstakingly well-groomed from the careful makeup on her face down to her finger and toenails. She often looked ready to be a news anchor, only somehow she managed to avoid working anywhere. Emma wasn't in touch with them, so maybe that had changed.

She said, "My stepmother's very attractive, so is my stepsister. And they can both be charming to outsiders. My dad was taken in, for sure."

At the word, "charming," Peter thought suddenly of Lila. Like Emma's stepfamily, she was attractive and had a kind of magnetic charm, the attention-getting kind. If there was a party, everyone knew Lila was there. If it was a dinner, she'd dominate the conversation.

It hadn't bothered him. He knew she wasn't the sweetest thing on two legs, but he'd never thought deeply enough about her character. She was fun and flirty and alluring. In the end, he was no different than Emma's father—he'd been taken in, too. It was his own fault for not choosing a girlfriend with more discretion. He looked at Emma, wondering if he was making the same mistake. They hadn't yet had the conversation necessary to know for sure, but she was certainly no Lila. There was quietness and humility about her. His hand came and covered one of hers. "I'm sorry."

She shook her head as if to shake off the memories. "It's okay." With a light in her eyes, she said softly, "Dad was great, otherwise. Before they married."

They made a turn and pulled up just ahead of the building on Rockefeller Plaza. The Rainbow Room was on the 65th floor, but the building was so tall Emma couldn't see the top from the car. Above the entrance was a huge marquee with neon lights that said, "Rainbow Room, Observation Deck." Below that was, "NBC Studios." Peter made no move to exit the limo.

Emma loved how he'd been listening closely and nodding from time to time. His deep blue eyes, when they looked into hers, revealed compassion that touched her heart. His hand, still upon hers, gave a squeeze.

What a wonderful night this was—if only. If Emma could forget the cloud of anxiety she'd been living in since the day Ricky dumped the burden on her. But she couldn't forget—she wasn't on a date with an impossibly perfect guy in order to enjoy him or it— she was on a mission to save the necks of herself and her family. The ever-present weight of it invaded everything. Even what lay ahead, a night in the exclusive Rainbow Room with Peter, felt shadowed, as if she could never fully participate, but stood like an outsider, looking in at what should have been a joy.

Until the burden of this weight was lifted, she could never be wholly present with Peter as she wanted. And unless she could find a way around needing help from him, she would feel dishonest and ashamed. Truth was, she'd gotten herself into an impossible situation. If anything had become clear over the course of their short time together, it was this: Peter Bentsen was someone she did not want to injure by lying to him, and certainly not by using him for money.

They continued talking. Emma wanted to raise the question that had served as the perfect reason to have dinner with Peter to begin with. What was last night really about from his perspective? She knew he was unaware of Ricky's scheme, but still wondered what he knew but thought she did not. Yet she'd keep her half of the bargain. He'd asked her to have dinner with him before he'd talk about it—she would do that. Then she'd ask questions.

He said, "Shall we go in? The party's in full swing by now. There'll be a small table ready for us, maybe in Bar 65."

Chapter Eleven

Emma wasn't the bar-hopping type but knew from pictures online that Bar 65 was really a lounge attached to the Rainbow Room and wouldn't be one of those places crowded with beer drinkers and TVs playing sports. Peter had class. They passed beneath the marquee and entered the building. Peter led them to an escalator that took them to the mezzanine. They joined another couple in glitzy evening wear at the elevator. Emma noted that Peter was by far the better-looking man. I'm being shallow! she scolded herself.

When they arrived, they entered a glittering ballroom with its famous circle of colored light—daylight blue at the moment—over the dancefloor, lending a light, airy feel to the room.

Massive floral arrangements in giant bronze urns flanked the entrance and dotted the room. Round dinner tables set with gleaming crystal and floral centerpieces made up the perimeter, while the four corners had gated, raised areas with more tables. Elegantly dressed guests circled each table, chattering busily. Behind them, a breathtaking view of New York City at night, sparkling as if starlit, filled the many windows.

Peter took her hand, and to her dismay, marched them right across the open dance floor in full view of everyone facing it. A momentary lull in conversation told Emma their presence was being observed. She figured Peter must be a sort of celebrity among the wealthy, as he wasn't only rich but exorbitantly rich. A rock star of the elite. Her stomach fluttered, but she tried to look calm, even casual, as though she was likely to be on the arm of such a man at any time.

A waiter came hurrying and greeted Peter with "Welcome back, sir, right this way, please." Peter stopped to wave and nod at a tuxedo-clad, middle-aged man at a raised table— the friend hosting the event, Emma gathered—who smiled and nodded, including an appreciative nod at Emma. They followed the waiter past the party and down a corridor to a small table at a wall of windows that included the glittering view of the city. It was almost dizzying. "The lounge is open to the public, but it's still quieter here than in the main room," he explained. Emma nodded, still taking in the view.

"Nice, right?" Peter said. "We'll take a peek from the Top of the Rock before we leave."

"The top of the rock?" she asked.

"The Observation Deck." He smiled and waved a hand at the panorama adjacent to them. "The view's even better than this."

"I'd like that," Emma said. Looking out at the city, she murmured, "It's beautiful." This is how the other half lives, she thought, taking in the fairy-tale view.

While a waiter came and filled their glasses, Peter named some of the taller buildings for her, pointing out the area right there in Midtown where his own offices were. Small dishes of something that looked like sushi were placed before them.

"I hope you don't mind," Peter said. "I called ahead and took the liberty of ordering this appetizer and our drink. This, and the rest of the menu are compliments of our host, Christopher Sostopheles, a business friend." He paused. "He's uh, a billionaire too." He lifted his glass and motioned for her to do likewise. "To Emma. On our first date. May there be many more." She smiled as their glasses touched. "Let me know how you like it," he said, raising the glass to his lips.

She took a sip. It was tangy but smooth and sweet. Very smooth. "It's great. Is this champagne?"

"One of the best." He paused and then added, watching for her reaction, "I only have one glass with a meal. One of any alcoholic beverage. I don't believe in drunkenness."

"I'm glad to hear that." Emma said. "I got drunk once in my teens and it was awful."

With a smile, he said, "I'm glad to hear *that.*"

He glanced at her plate. "I hope you like sashimi. It's wonderful here."

Emma hesitated. "I've never had it." She looked up with a sparkle in her eye. "But I'm willing to try it." It turned out that sashimi and champagne tasted excellent together.

As they ate and spoke, Peter behaved as though they had
the place to themselves. She listened with rapt attention while
he spoke about himself, but now and then other guests would
wander past, all dressed in attire that suggested class and taste.
Often, a loud phrase or sentence in a foreign language would
chance their way, and she'd listen and wonder at the country of
origin.

He must have seen her wandering gaze. "Is everything okay?"

She smiled. "I'm just gawking. I told you I'd probably
embarrass you the first chance I get."

He said patiently, "You are not an embarrassment. Quite the
contrary."

Waiters brought their dinner, and Emma's taste buds popped
with new flavors, beginning with "Maine Diver Scallop Baked
in its Shell" with chard, leeks, mushroom, and truffle, along
with "Oysters Rockefeller." Emma followed Peter's lead
and ate only enough to enjoy the flavor and texture of each
appetizer. Their entrees were "Crisp Long Island Roasted
Duck," and "Beef Wellington," which was prime tenderloin.
Each came with accompaniments such as "Orange Braised
Endive," "Potato Confit Leg Terrine," "Wild Mushrooms,"
"Parsnip," "Foie Gras Potato Puree," and "Sauce Perigord."

Peter told her more about his upbringing as the only son
of a retail magnate and how he'd had to work his way up the
corporate ladder like anyone else. When he was in school, his
grades had to be stellar for him to even earn an allowance.
After working in the shoe department, he did stints in other
departments. His dad said it would help him understand how
the store worked, and give him empathy for the working man

and woman. He admitted, however, that after college his path to becoming the CEO of Bentsen Global Associates had been fast. His father's heart attack three years ago had clinched it, at which point he stepped fully into his dad's shoes.

Now she understood how a billionaire could be so down-to-earth and not spoiled.

He took a sip of water, licked his lips and leveled his gaze upon Emma. Peter had a way of making her feel like no one else was in the room, giving her his full, deeply interested attention.

"I want to hear more about you." He smiled gently. "What are you studying in school?"

"English, with a minor in Fine Art." She gave a wry smile. "Spring term just finished which is why I'm free to go out again tonight."

He smiled. "Lucky for me. Then his brows furrowed. "How do you go to school and work full time?"

"School's at night. Sometimes on Saturdays too." She frowned. "That's the only thing I hate about it. Going at night." Her eyes clouded. "I'm not brave. I don't like walking on campus at night. I shudder every time I have to change buildings."

He frowned. "I don't blame you."

"I used to call Ricky while I was heading to the bus."

His brows creased. "That's right, you don't drive. Why not?"

Emma blushed. "I don't have a license." To his look of unbelief, she cried, "I grew up taking public transportation. And I can't afford a car, anyway. The insurance alone would be too much on my salary." She paused. "But I hate waiting at empty bus stops. I have to take two buses from school to get to my apartment."

He looked bothered, but then smiled suddenly. "I see some good times in our future. I'm going to teach you to drive."

Smiling, she bit her lip. "You would do that?"

"Not with the Lamborghini." He grinned. "But I'd enjoy it. Ricky should have offered." He immediately regretted mentioning her boyfriend. He didn't want her mind on Ricky.

"I never thought to ask him," Emma said.

He wanted to say, "You didn't ask me, either," but he was afraid it would put her on the defense for Ricky.

She wiped her mouth delicately and met his gaze. "So, tell me what you know about last night."

He smirked. "Tell me more about you, first."

"You said if I had dinner with you, you would explain to me about last night."

"And I will. I promise I will before I take you home. But right now I want to hear about you." When she was silent, wondering what to tell, he asked, "When did you lose your mom—your real mom?"

"When I was seven."

"So it was only you and your dad for a long time."

She nodded. "The good old days."

"Tell me again why your stepfamily didn't like you?"

She shook her head. "I don't know. I think they felt my father loved me more or something. And actually, it became that way because they treated me so badly. But it didn't start out that way."

Peter nodded, his eyes thoughtful. "I have a theory."

"About?"

"Why they didn't like you."

She smiled. "Let's hear it."

He motioned with his arm. "Without knowing anything more about it, or them, I'm willing to guess your step-sister doesn't approach you in looks. You're beautiful, and they couldn't stomach it."

She smiled, but with a shadow of sadness about her mouth. "They are both very attractive women."

"As attractive as you?" he returned quickly, smiling.

"I could find them on Facebook if you like."

"No need. I'm sticking with my theory."

She smiled, reflecting that although Peter's theory was incorrect, it was sweet of him to assume what he had. And he'd called her beautiful again. The night was going as smoothly as clockwork. If only she could level with Peter and tell him everything!

Music started up from the ballroom and he said, "I'm looking forward to our dance."

Emma blushed. Maybe it was the champagne. Or maybe it was the "I'm looking forward to it" part that infused her cheeks with color.

Just then a waiter came and said, "Sir. Mr. Sostopheles asks you to stop by his table."

Peter said, "Of course. As soon as we're finished eating."

Emma was finished and told him so, though she was nervous about meeting Mr. Sostopheles. Peter quickly scooped up a last bite, chewed it down and took a sip of his drink. He wiped his mouth with a cloth napkin. "C'mon, let's say hi."

Emma said, as she rose, "I have to meet another billionaire?"

Peter tucked her arm within his. "No worries—he's a normal guy."

"Just a normal guy with a billion dollars in the bank," she said snidely.

He chuckled. "It doesn't work that way. Most of the money's in assets."

As they kept moving, he leaned toward her and said with a wink, "He's probably asking us over because he caught sight of you."

"I doubt that," she said, but fresh nervous flutters swept through her. She fought the urge to do more gawking as they joined the guests, not wanting to advertise that it was her first time in the posh eatery.

Christopher Sostopheles stood to greet Peter with a smile, exchanging a firm handshake. Peter introduced Emma as his date, and the man turned and took her hands, proclaimed it a pleasure to meet Peter's lovely companion, then gave her a quick peck on the cheek. He thanked them for coming and introduced Emma to his soon-to-be bride Elitsa, a classical, super-model beauty. Peter greeted her as Christopher had greeted Emma, taking her hands with a warm smile and a peck on the cheek. They exchanged quick pleasantries, enough for Emma to know they were already acquainted. Peter then turned to Christopher to chat. Elitsa smiled warmly at Emma, who felt too shy to do more than return a weak smile of her own.

"How do you know Pe-ter?" she asked, in what seemed a charming eastern European accent.

"We have a mutual friend who introduced us," Emma said.

Elitsa nodded. "Friends are good. That's how I met Chris."

Emma found her tongue and congratulated her on her coming nuptials.

"You and Pe-ter must come," she said. "The ceremony will be in Greece, but we'll be back in New York for a celebration shortly afterward." She glanced at Peter and said, "Who knows? Pe-ter may decide to join us in Greece for the ceremony. If he does, he must bring you. But with him, you never know."

"No?" Emma was curious what she meant by that.

"He does not travel on Sundays like most businessmen," she said with amusement. "So sometimes he won't come to events on a Saturday; if he's got pressing business on Monday in New York, for example."

Emma nodded. Hadn't Sy said Peter was religious? Could that be why he didn't travel on Sundays? It seemed a bit extreme.

Soon, Christopher announced that he was going to dance with his fiancée, and they parted cordially, both graciously saying how nice it was to meet Emma. "They are soooo nice!" Emma said into his ear, afterward.

Peter nodded. "Good people." He took her hand. "Let's take a quick look from the Observation Deck, and then we'll join the dance floor." She noticed that he often told her what they'd do, not asked her. But she figured a guy with so much money and power was used to doing what he wanted, and what he wanted was usually something good, something she'd agree with. She nodded and smiled. "I'd love to."

They turned to retrace their steps to Bar 65, which led to the Observation Deck.

Passing their table, he spotted their half-finished glasses of champagne. "Let's finish our drinks, first, if you don't mind." Emma agreed but excused herself to use the restroom.

Seconds after she walked off, a new party was seated within Peter's view. The moment he recognized the woman who sat down, she looked up and met his eyes—Lila! She gasped, said something to the man she was with and rose to head his way. The man with her swiveled around to get a look at Peter, while Lila paraded her way over, flipping her long hair behind one shoulder. With a smile that didn't match her eyes, she arrived and glanced over the table, taking in that he wasn't alone.

"I'm busy," Peter said.

"Hello to you, too!" Her eyes widened with indignation.

"OK. Hello. I hope you're well. Have a good night."

"When did you get mean? You used to be such a nice guy. I was always bragging about how nice a guy you were!"

He cleared his throat. "You were always bragging about something else if memory serves. Something you liked more than 'nice.'" His eyes narrowed as he spoke.

Her face fell. "How many times do I have to tell you? I was angry because I thought you were stupid to risk everything on one deal like Sy told me. It made me feel insecure."

"Stop right now."

She continued, "It wasn't the money. I was upset. I admit I wasn't thinking of your feelings. I acted in anger. I've apologized numerous times."

"And I accepted your apology. Can we move on, now?"

"If you really accepted it, we could start over," she said with a tragic air.

He said nothing, just tightened his lips.

She glanced at Emma's plate. "Are you with a woman?"

"Is that your business?"

She swallowed. "I still have feelings for you. Yes, I feel like it is my business."

"Spare me, Lila, please."

She blinked back tears.

"Oh, here we go," he said, leaning back in his seat in annoyance. "Please return to your date and leave me in peace."

Her lips firmed into a line. She turned to go, but suddenly froze. Her mouth hung open. "Emma? Here? What is *she* doing here?"

Peter followed her gaze and saw Emma coming back. She looked so appealing in the gold sequined dress. It was modest and yet hugged her slim curves enough to reveal her beauty. She walked with class, tall and straight, but without a hint of hauteur. He liked that. She'd been looking at the view through the windows, but she turned her head and smiled at Peter. Then, right before his eyes, the smile froze on her lips when she saw Lila glaring at her. She slowed her steps.

"You know her?" Peter asked.

Lila turned to him with a look of outrage. "Know her? That's my stepsister! The little Queens rat! Remember I told you how my family had to move to Queens and put up with—her? Her and her father—he was a con job and so is she!"

Peter stood up. "You should go."

She tossed her head. "After I ask her what she's doing here."

"No, you'll go now, Lila, or I'll call security." His voice was edged with ice. "Emma is here because she came with me. She's my date."

Chapter Twelve

Lila gasped, blinking, and gripped the top of Emma's chair to steady herself. Struggling to speak, her jaw worked silently until finally she sputtered, "YOU are with Emma? I don't believe this! Did you do this just to spite me?"

Peter had taken on a look that approached compassion as he saw Lila's reaction, but now the blue eyes were daggers. "Don't be ridiculous. I had no idea of your relationship."

Emma arrived and Lila motioned at her. "But SHE did! I'll bet she got hold of you just to spite me!"

Emma looked frightened and confused. "You know my stepsister?" she asked Peter.

"As if you didn't know!" Lila spat out.

Emma just blinked at her. Lila turned to Peter.

"She's—she's taking advantage of you!" In one quick movement, she grabbed Emma's ice water and tossed the contents at Emma. It hit her face, neck and bodice, but as she gasped from the cold and blinked water out of her eyes, she felt drops of cold liquid dripping from her hair too.

Peter had to use every ounce of self-control not to shake Lila physically. Fortunately, there wasn't a full house in the Lounge, but the area fell silent as a waiter came hurrying up and apologized profusely while offering Emma a dazzlingly white serving towel to dry herself off with. Seconds later a restaurant dignitary hurried over and motioned to Lila's date. Turning to Lila he said, "You will leave. Now. Mr. Bentsen is our valued friend and you have insulted him and his companion."

"She insulted me first!" cried Lila. Ignoring her, he nodded at an approaching security guard, who took Lila's arm. She tried to shake herself free but failed. Peter took the towel from Emma and dabbed gently at her face and hair. Lila watched him tearfully as she was escorted off. Peter's eyes met hers. "You're a lunatic," he said. "Someone ought to lock you up."

Emma was mortified. It wasn't every day she came to the poshest restaurant she'd ever been in only to have her stepsister throw a glass of ice water on her. She dried herself off as much as she could, surprised and pleased to find the sequins on her dress repelled water. Swanky clothing had its perks.

The fabric beneath still felt damp, though, as did some of her hair, and definitely her spirits. Peter said, placing her wrap about her shoulders, "We'll come another time for the Observation Deck. I imagine you're ready to go."

Emma nodded gratefully. "I'm sorry."

"I am too, about Lila." He called for the car and then took Emma's hand to leave. He'd looked forward to the intimacy of holding her in his arms while dancing, but that could wait. He gave her a look filled with compassion. "I knew she had a temper, but I never dreamed she'd act out that way." He led them around the crowded dance floor, taking a cursory look for Christopher to thank him before leaving. He and Elitsa were nowhere in sight, probably in the center of the dancers.

Emma took a last look at the glowing city through the windows. She hadn't thought to get a single picture. "How do you know Lila?" she asked, as they exited to wait for an elevator. She was still processing the shock of not only seeing her stepsister but of discovering that Peter knew her.

His lips compressed in a line. "I used to date her." But he searched her face a moment. "You didn't know?"

She shook her head. "I had no idea! After I moved out, they dropped me completely. They hardly even send a Christmas card, though I send them one every year. We don't spend holidays together and I only visited the house once since I left." She looked down. "I could tell I wasn't wanted." She shook her head again. "I can't believe that you dated her! No wonder she was so angry. She must hate me more than ever."

He met her eyes. "I'm sorry about that. I hate to be the cause of further…family discord."

She smiled sadly. "We were never really family, so don't worry about that." The elevator arrived and they got on, the sole occupants. Emma's brows furrowed. "I hope she doesn't start sending me hate mail. Or mean texts or phone calls."

"Let me know if she does," he said, his eyes hard and glittering.

Minutes later they were back in the limo, moving slowly through traffic. They were leaving through a different route than the one they'd taken earlier. Between roadwork, pedestrians, and red lights, their headway was slow. New York after 10:30 pm was no less busy than it had been earlier. Emma shivered involuntarily. Peter removed his white jacket and placed it over her shoulder wrap, then slid closer to put an arm about her.

"Thank you," Emma said, noting how warm and caring his eyes were. She held his gaze, knowing she ought to look away, she ought to send the message that he had to keep his distance. But Peter was awesome. She felt safe with him and had visions of telling him her whole sordid story before the night ended. He was trustworthy, Sofia said. And Emma had seen nothing to make her think otherwise. Despite Ricky's threat, heaven had put Peter in her path, and he was crazy wonderful.

Peter's head moved closer; her lips parted, but suddenly he sat up and looked past her out the window. She bit her lip. He didn't want to kiss her.

They turned onto Second Avenue, and he said, "We're taking the tunnel back because it's faster. You see how busy this is? It looks just like this at 2 am. I once came through at 4 am and it was still busy, people hanging out with cigarettes on their front stoops, every traffic light with a crowd waiting to cross."

Emma nodded. The sheer number of pedestrians amazed her. A mounted police officer went past, the horse evidently used to the bustle, horns, and throngs of people. "There's a reason it's called the city that never sleeps!" she said. Taking a deep breath, she asked, "So what happened between you and Lila?"

He sighed. "We only dated for about two months. Then she broke up with me."

Emma's brows rose. "She broke up with you?"

He nodded, while a little smirk played at the sides of his mouth.

Emma said, "Well, she obviously has regrets, doesn't she?"

His brows came together. "Crocodile tears. But I'm still very sorry about her behavior. I feel awful!"

"It wasn't your fault. That's just how she is."

Peter turned to her. "I should tell you why she broke up with me."

Emma listened curiously. "I wondered about that." Lila loved to live it up. Emma couldn't understand why she'd let go of a catch like Peter.

He nodded. "Sure. I don't want you to think it was due to bad behavior on my part."

"I would find that hard to believe," she said, smiling gently.

He squeezed her shoulder. "Thanks. Here's what happened. Sy, for some unfathomable reason, told her one day that I'd lost everything in a disastrous business deal." He paused.

"He was joking, of course. And a smarter woman might have known to question that, but she bought the story and within the hour called me up. I couldn't take her call at the time, and she left me a message that we were through."

Emma's eyes rounded in indignation for Peter, and amazement that even Lila would be that callous. "She likes nice things, but I didn't think she was that materialistic."

"Neither did I." He gazed at her soberly. "Unfortunately, she hid her true character."

Emma's heart sank and she shuddered inwardly. She was doing the exact same thing!

Peter leaned his head toward hers, closer than before. "That's one thing I really like about you. I feel I know you, and I trust you."

Emma's heart became a thousand-pound weight. It was the weight that would send her to the bottom of the Hudson, and her family, because now she knew she could never reveal what she needed from Peter. He'd take her for another Lila!

Peter, watching her reaction, continued, "I already know, thanks to Ricky, that you aren't after the biggest prize and you won't sell yourself for money."

"Thanks to Ricky?"

He moved his head away. "OK. What you wanted to know about what really happened last night…He paused. "Why don't you tell me first what you thought was happening?"

A surge of alarm made her counter with, "No, you promised to tell me. It doesn't matter what I thought. You said there was something Ricky would never tell me. What is it?"

Peter sighed. "Ok. I have mixed feelings about this because I wouldn't have met you if not for Ricky.

But he didn't want me at that party to keep you company while he was busy. He's got a lot of wealth, apparently, and thought you might be onto it—and after it." Concerned eyes studied her.

Emma said, "Oh, Sofia told me something to that effect."

"Sofia told you?"

"Well, she said Ricky was testing my loyalty with you, because you're so good-looking." She smiled sheepishly.

Peter kissed her lips quickly, but then said, "That wasn't it, though. He thought you were a fortune hunter. I hate to say it this way, but he was really testing whether you'd stick with him or go for me because I'm wealthier than he is."

Emma sat back as if this was a shock. "That snake." It was easy to say that because Ricky was one. She turned wounded eyes to Peter. "But I did go for you. So he thinks I'm a fortune hunter." And he would be right, she thought sadly. He'd turned her into one.

Peter stroked the side of her face. "Don't worry about it. I know you're not."

Emma's heart ached at his words. How she wished they were true!

He studied her. "You must be very hurt by Ricky. Honestly, I can't think highly of him. You dated for weeks but he still suspected you. I've only known you for days and I know already how wrong he is." He leaned over and kissed her, a warm, sweet, kiss.

Afterward, she stifled tears. Peter was great—she was falling fast for him! But she couldn't help but think that the sweet kiss they just shared was for her the kiss of death. She could never ask him for money.

If she did, it would break her heart because she'd have to disillusion him, to show him that he was wrong, and she was just like her stepsister.

Sooner or later the mob would find out and come for her and the others.

They were dead meat. It was inevitable.

Chapter Thirteen

At the door to her apartment, to her surprise Peter asked, "Do you attend a church?"

Emma shook her head. "I did before I moved out on my own, but once I started working full-time, which at first included Sundays, I just never got around to finding a new one."

He nodded. "I'd like to take you to mine sometime." He paused. "May I ask? Do you consider yourself a Christian?"

"Of course!" She was surprised at such a question.

"So, you'll come with me sometime?"

"Sure! I miss church. Some." She smiled.

He went to kiss her. "That's honest."

After a brief kiss, they said their goodnights, Peter adding that he'd call her the next afternoon.

Emma went downstairs brimming with mixed feelings. Peter was sweet and kind and it only made her feel worse! What a mess she was in. It had been a wonderful night with him until Lila showed up, but somehow Peter had made it wonderful again. Until he told her about his breakup. Why was it that her stepsister was still a bane of her existence? How completely uncanny it was that Lila had dated him, and not only that, but muddied the waters for Emma so that she couldn't ask Peter for help. It wasn't fair!

While she changed into PJs and then removed her makeup, she figured that maybe one day she would be able to approach Peter with her need. If he really cared for her, perhaps he'd understand that she wasn't like Lila at all. Lila had pretended to be one thing when she was another. Emma had also hidden the truth, but only for survival—and now for Peter's protection, if Ricky was right that no amount of money would keep him safe from the mob "enforcers." But if she didn't risk asking him, her only other choice was to finagle some kind of legal commitment from him and then demand the money! She couldn't imagine doing it. She'd never commit herself to him unless he knew the situation. With despair, she realized it was a catch-22 and she went to bed utterly disheartened, her energy spent.

Peter called Emma late the following afternoon. Nadia and Chris were visiting, and Nadia's eyes lit after the phone buzzed and Emma told her it was him.

"Put it on speaker!" she hissed, but Emma shooed her away.

Nadia put up water for jasmine tea, but she kept looking back at Emma, who could see she was listening. Chris was putting out dishes for the Chinese take-out food they'd ordered.

"Tuesday evening?" Emma asked. "Yes, I can."

In the kitchenette, Nadia wrung her hands to keep from squealing.

Emma said, "Casual? Are you sure?" Then, "It's a surprise? Uh-oh."

At the other end, Peter said, "I promise, it's nothing extravagant. I just want to see you again."

"Okay. But if you take me somewhere ritzy, I won't go in. I'm already the fish out of water meeting your friends."

"No worries," he said.

Emma chatted with Peter for a few minutes longer, then thanked him for calling and said she was looking forward to seeing him. Nadia could hardly contain herself and was at Emma's side as soon as she'd thumbed off the call.

"I told you!" she exclaimed happily. "It's love!"

Emma frowned. "Will you stop that? It'll only be our second date."

"But the third time you've seen each other. And he called you today right after seeing you last night! It's love." She turned to Chris. "Don't you think it's love, hon?" When he looked up and nodded obediently, she clapped her hands together and put her head against them. "I knew you'd find someone wonderful!"

"Slow down," Emma said, getting annoyed. "Peter is not someone to joke about."

"I'm not joking," Nadia said, in a much more sober tone.

"Well, this isn't a lighthearted relationship," Emma explained.

"No, it's the love of your life relationship," Nadia said, suppressing a smile. "Peter is going to help you and get you out of trouble, and then he'll want to marry you."

"And just why would he want to do those things?" Emma asked, grabbing the bowls that Chris forgot to put out for the Won-Ton soup.

Nadia smiled calmly. "Because it's love."

Emma shook her head, but she had an idea and grinned mischievously. Loudly, she said, "So why aren't you two married?"

Chris's head popped up from where he sat using his phone. He watched Nadia as if to see how she'd answer, but she only turned and stared at him with a little frown. "Ask Chris," she said. Emma looked at Chris, but he shrugged his shoulders as if to say, "Beats me."

He's clueless, Emma thought.

While they ate, she told them in more detail what had happened with Lila, and why she could never ask Peter to help her now. "He'll see me as just another Lila," she said, sadly.

Nadia disagreed vehemently. Emma said, "Chris, what would you think if you were Peter, and on our second date, I told you I needed a hundred thousand bucks. And Lila broke up with you because of money and she's my stepsister."

Chris's cute, meaty .face scrunched in thought. "Well…I guess…I wouldn't give it to you."

Nadia stared at him like he had two heads, and then smacked his arm. "You're not helping! Of course, you would give it to her! You're a billionaire in love, remember?"

"Well, yeah, um, then I'd give it to her," he amended.

Emma groaned. "Stop calling it love! If anyone's in love, it's me—" She froze, embarrassed. "I mean, if anyone falls in love, it would be me before him. He's great—I'm just me. Needy me."

Nadia said, "If he's not in love with you, he will be, Em."

Dryly, Emma returned, "Oh, like the way Ricky fell for me?"

"Ricky is, like… an alien," Nadia said. "He's not normal." She took a bite of food and added, "None of those men in the mob are normal. I mean, you saw *The Godfather*, right? They just kill each other all the time."

Emma frowned. "And those who don't pay them back, apparently."

Nadia said, "They won't kill you. They want the dough. And you have Peter."

Ricky called that night. "How did it go on Saturday night?"

She glared at the phone because she couldn't glare at Ricky. "It went well."

"Any progress?"

"I'm seeing him again on Tuesday night. Like I said, it's going well."

"What will you be doing with him?"

"I'm not sure yet."

"Okay," Ricky said. "Keep me posted on any good news."

She was about to thumb off, but he said, "And Emma—"

"Yes?"

"They've got a tail on Adam. Just in case."

"I hate you!" Sudden tears filled her eyes.

"Don't blame me, blame your father."

She ended the call.

By the next morning, she'd calmed down. She'd spoken to Adam and tried to subtly warn him to stay in public places, though he made no promises. Adam, like Emma, wasn't the life of the party; he liked being alone and left to study quietly. He sometimes hung out with his roommate and another friend who shared his interests and were as studious as he. Emma's worries seemed to amuse him, but he assured her his college was safe, especially for a guy.

Tuesday came quickly. All day, Emma fluttered between excitement and nervous anticipation to see Peter again. He greeted her at the door with a quick peck on the lips. At the curb, instead of a limo, a sleek black car awaited them with a man at the wheel. He jumped out and opened the back door for them.

"So you have normal cars, too," she said, smiling, as Peter helped her get in before him.

He grinned.

Emma immediately realized she'd been wrong. Instead of the usual back seat space, the trunk of the car appeared to have been shortened to give twice the leg room, and the seats were custom fit with gorgeous deep tan leather softer than her upholstered sofa.

"I take that back, this isn't normal," she said, as he got in beside her. In front of her was more luxury customization with a charging station for multiple devices, and other gadgets.

He said, "It's comfortable. I like good cars." But he turned to her while buckling his seat belt. "I'm not a spendthrift about everything, though. And I support dozens of charities personally, besides what we do through the department store and other affiliates."

Bentsen's Department Store, she recalled, was well-known for its many outreaches into communities and for supporting everything from Special Olympics to children's hospitals.

"I'm glad," she said, sincerely.

"I know where my wealth comes from," he said, philosophically. "I'd have nothing if God didn't see fit to give it to me."

"That's a good way to look at it," she said, also sincerely.

"It's the right way," he returned. "Every good gift comes from God."

Emma nodded. She'd never thought about it that way, but it made sense. God controlled everything, didn't he? *Please, God, help me!* She didn't pray often, and it wasn't much of a prayer, but Peter's words reminded her that, if anyone could help her, it was God. Considering her circumstances, it seemed only God could. She liked that Peter was religious.

Once again, they approached the 59th Street Bridge with the city looming ahead. It wasn't as impressive a view as after sunset, but still was interesting. Emma never failed to be stirred by the thought of how much humanity inhabited all those skyscrapers. She glanced up, but there was no sunroof.

She said with a smile, "We're going to the city again?"

He nodded. "To a nice, cozy place for a quiet dinner in Washington Square. I hope you like Italian?"

"Love it," she said, belatedly realizing that Ricky was Italian and she ought to wash her hands of everything that reminded her of him. But did she really want to give up Italian food? No. She said, "Twice in one week to Manhattan! Nadia will envy me."

He smiled at this since he was there at least five days a week. "Is Nadia a good friend?"

"The best. We've known each other since junior high. Her and her boyfriend Chris are like family to me."

"I'm very glad you have them." His earnest blue eyes upon her made her feel again like Peter had nothing else in the world to occupy him except her. Even Ricky's thoughtful gaze upon her when they'd talked while dating didn't match Peter's attentiveness. Perhaps it was because Ricky's attention wasn't whole-hearted. He got to know Emma only so that he could collect a debt for his underhanded bosses. Peter's attention was genuine.

They were dropped off in front of Carbone's on Thompson Street. To Emma's relief, a couple entering ahead of them looked like ordinary people and weren't dressed up. She and Peter stood in line behind them for the maître d', when a man in a shirt and tie came speedily out of nowhere to greet Peter. "Mr. Bentsen! Welcome, welcome!" he exclaimed effusively but in hushed tones to them. "We are ready for you, if you will follow me, please."

They were escorted past a half-filled dining area and another, emptier one before being ushered into a small offshoot room with a table set for two. The room was windowless but pretty landscape paintings graced the walls, and a floral centerpiece and candlelight on the table lent an intimate, cozy air.

"What's your favorite Italian dish?" Peter asked when they were seated. A waiter filled their water glasses, while another opened a bottle of red wine and poured each glass half full.

"Eggplant Rollatini," Emma said without hesitation.

A third waiter brought in a tray of appetizers. Peter stopped him before he left and said, "Can we get Eggplant Rollatini also?"

The waiter bowed his head. "It's a plain dish, sir, not on our menu, but I'll see what I can do."

"Please," Peter said.

Emma blushed. How gauche she must seem. But Peter said, "It's only as plain as the chef who makes it, right?"

Emma smiled gratefully. He was so kind. She looked at the spread. "Dinner with you means instant service, I see."

"I asked them to start us quickly," he explained. "I'm sort of on a schedule."

Emma smirked in mock reproval. "Do you always follow a schedule when you're not working and on your own time?"

He looked speechless for a moment. "Not really. Do I have a general idea of how I want things to go, timewise? Yes. But I'm not a fanatic about it."

Emma smiled. "Well, if you were, I could say I finally found something negative about you."

He grinned. "I'm sure you'll find plenty as you get to know me." He motioned at the food but said, "Do you mind if I say a blessing before we eat?"

"Not at all." She followed Peter's lead and bowed her head. He gave thanks to God for the meal and asked a blessing over it. He added, "And please bless our time together. Amen."

Emma found it touching that he'd included their time together in his prayer. As they picked at the appetizers, he named them, "Carpacio Piemontese," "Calamari Marco," and "Prosciutto & Mozzarella."

"Why don't you tell me something negative about you so I don't have to feel like I'm with Mr. Perfect."

He smiled. "Mr. Perfect, huh? Hmmm, you're definitely wrong there. But do I have to tell you something negative about me? I'm not sure I want to pop your bubble."

"Please," she returned. "I feel like—well, you know how in the bird world a male bird usually has all the beautiful coloring and the females are often plain and drab?"

He nodded.

"Well, to me, that's us. You're like a superstar of the rich, full of color and interesting, and I'm plain Jane."

His brows shot up. "That is so not accurate. You're quieter than I am, but you are the beautiful one, and I find you extremely interesting." He sipped his wine. "We're not a pair of birds. The way I see it, you are Cinderella, and I'm," he cleared his throat, and repressed a grin, "your Prince Charming."

Emma grinned. "You certainly are! Perfect Prince Charming. Tell me something not perfect about you." A waiter came in carrying platters of steaming dishes which were placed in the center between them. Since Peter had apparently ordered beforehand, he again gave the name of each dish. "Jumbo Shrimp Scampi," "Lobster Fra Diavolo," "Veal Marsala" and "Cherry Pepper Ribs." Before he left he said, with a small bow, "Eggplant Rollatini is underway."

"Thank you," Peter said. "Well done."

Looking at all the food, Emma was embarrassed that yet more was coming, and because of her preference. "This is so much food," she said.

Peter smiled. "Let's dig in."

Before they left the restaurant, Peter texted his driver so that the car awaited them at the street. They left with a bagful of take-home containers which Peter insisted were all for Emma, despite her protests. He was extravagant about ordering. Happily, he'd tried the eggplant dish and seemed to genuinely like it. He told her it was a good choice. She couldn't tell if he was just being nice.

He hadn't answered her question as to something negative about him save for the common male bugaboos of not being the neatest, not cooking much, and, unlike many men, he didn't enjoy outdoor sports except Mets baseball and tennis. He had a box at Citi Field.

Emma cried, "I love baseball! I'm a Mets fan, too."

Peter smiled. "Perfect. We'll go to some games together." He gave her a sideways look. "And I'll introduce you to tennis."

The car slowed and she looked out and saw Central Park. At the curb ahead of them was a white horse attached to a sweet old-fashioned buggy. The horse's mane shone beneath the streetlight, rich and noble. It wouldn't have surprised her had it been a unicorn.

"C'mon, Cinderella," Peter said. "Let's take a fairy tale ride with a white horse through the park."

Emma hesitated. It sounded wonderful, but from what she could see of the road into the park, it looked dark and foreboding in there.

"At night?"

He nodded. "Don't worry. It's a good section of the park."

"But it's dark in there," she said, peering past him into a shadowed paved lane.

"It's safe, I promise."

"You've done this before?"

"A long time ago. But people do it every night. I think the driver's armed."

As she allowed him to hand her from the car, she said, "You probably say that to comfort all your girls."

He grinned a disarming smile. "I don't go out with a lot of girls. That was part of my upbringing too, I guess."

She turned to him, marveling. "You had an incredible father."

"And mother."

Emma turned and bit her lip, falling silent. Peter took her hand and led her to the horse and buggy, paid the man, and helped her up into the seat with its canopy covering.

As they clip-clopped into the park, Peter put a protective arm about her. She enjoyed his nearness and the swaying feel of the vehicle. She tried to swallow her fears. She wasn't alone, and Peter was no wimp. Still, would he be equal to a mugger? To a possible band of muggers? She couldn't help but wonder and kept looking around uneasily.

"Are you frightened?"

"A little," she admitted.

He gently drew her closer and said in a sweet, low voice, "I'll protect you!"

Despite wondering how exactly he might do that if the need arose, Emma felt her heart warm, her fears melt away. Peter Bentsen was truly a sweetheart. How incredibly foolish Lila was, to break up with him. Emma was still trying to wrap her head around the fact that of all the women in New York, he'd dated her stepsister. And she couldn't understand how Lila—or anyone, for that matter—would break up with Peter over money. She'd be falling for Peter were he a typical working man, even one short on cash or living paycheck to paycheck. The limo and other perks of his wealth were fun, but he himself was the best thing about it all.

It hit her with fresh angst how unfair it was that Lila had dropped him because she thought he'd gone broke. It was impossible now for Emma to tell Peter what she desperately needed. Her stepsister had brought nothing but pain into Emma's life and was still managing to do so.

Riding through the park in the cozy buggy and with his arm about her, she longed to tell him the truth and face the consequences. But what if she lost him by telling him? Lila's accusation from the other night rang in Emma's mind, loud and clear. "She's taking advantage of you!" Would Peter agree with that if she asked him for help?

After the sweet buggy ride, they left the city along roads Emma quickly lost track of and didn't recognize. She could see they were headed back toward the Island, though. He was taking her home. Every cell in her body went into high alert. If she were going to tell Peter the truth, it had to be soon. The longer she waited, the more he would doubt her veracity.

Tonight, she felt close to him. She wanted to believe that he would trust her. And that, even if he turned down her request, he'd be kind about it. That he'd help her find a different solution to the problem. She wanted to believe that he could maybe even pull strings and get the mob off her back, no payment required. She wanted to believe it.

But what seemed most likely, most real, was that he'd realize what a phony she'd been. He'd drop her as quickly as Lila had dropped him.

No, Emma couldn't say a word.

Chapter Fourteen

Emma's phone rang at seven-thirty, just as she was scrambling to get ready for work.

"How'd it go last night?" It was Ricky, his voice flat and heavy.

"I can't talk now. I'll call you when I'm on my lunch break."

"How'd it go?" Now he sounded insistent and mean.

"Fine. It went fine."

"They're badgering me about you, Emma."

"I know that, Ricky—just please get off my back, okay? I will call you when I know there's something good to report."

"Are you getting closer?"

She hesitated. "Yes." Emma had no choice but to lie. She didn't feel anywhere near closer to getting the money, although she did feel closer to Peter.

"How close?"

"This isn't a science!" she cried. "This kind of thing takes time. I'm closer, okay? I can't say exactly how or when I will get what you want."

"When will you see him again?"

"Friday night."

"Good. But get the lead out, Emma. The family is breathing down my neck and it's all I can do to keep your brother safe."

Emma gasped and hung up. She called Adam with a pounding heart.

"Why are you calling me this early?" he asked. "I'm getting ready for my first class."

She could tell he was yawning. "Is everything okay? Anything weird happening?"

"Like what? What do you think is gonna happen? Why do you ask me these weird questions every time you call?"

"I don't know. But have you noticed any strange people watching you?"

"What're you talking about? This place is full of strange people. I'm probably one of them."

He hadn't noticed anything, good. "Okay, kiddo. Just stay alert, okay? I'll talk to you later."

Adam probably thought she was the strangest of all, calling to check on him with odd questions. She made a cup of coffee, got dressed, and put on makeup. When she left the house, she locked the door and headed down the walkway to the street, adjusting the jacket of her pantsuit. She nearly bumped into someone at the gate. She looked up to stare in shock at the face of Peter Bentsen, smiling gently.

"Peter!"

"Surprise," he said. He leaned in and gave her a kiss on the cheek. "I am your chauffeur this morning," he said, in a mock British accent. "To City Hospital, is that correct?"

She was speechless a moment, still trying to take in the fact that Peter was there to give her a lift to work! *Oh, my gosh. This man was an angel!* She nodded, and managed to say, "Yes, thank you!"

At the curb was a sleek black sports car. He opened the door for her and then went around to the driver's side.

"Is this your Lamborghini?" she asked, after he was seated behind the driver's seat.

"No way. This is a McLaren F1. The Lamborghini costs nearly twice as much as this."

He started the engine. "You'll have to tell me the way to your hospital."

"I'll be early if we go now. Buses take longer than a car."

His eyes sparkled at her. "That's great! That gives us time—" he pulled away from the curb. "For your first driving lesson."

She swallowed. "In this fancy car? Don't risk it on me."

He grinned. "I came prepared to risk it. But don't worry. Tell me where to find a big empty parking lot or something like that."

She couldn't think of where to find a big parking lot that would be empty, so she had him head for Malba, the upper-class neighborhood where Ricky lived and the streets were quiet. On second thought, she didn't want to be close to the snake. She directed him back to a professional neighborhood in Flushing. It wasn't as ritzy or quiet but would do.

The car drove as smoothly as riding on a cloud, even despite a few pot-hole-ridden streets. How could she dare take a lesson in it? She said, "You're very sweet to offer, but it's too early for me to learn. I need more coffee for that." She smiled. "Thank you for the opportunity, but could we talk, instead? We could grab a quick cup of coffee or something."

Peter studied her. "Are you afraid of driving?"

"I'm afraid of driving this car, yes."

He shook his head.

Quickly she added, "We don't have much time, anyway. Let's grab a coffee and then we can sit near the hospital in the car until I have to go in."

He nodded. "As you wish."

Twelve minutes later, sitting in a "NO PARKING" spot, the only empty one they found, they sat facing each other. "We're not parked," Peter explained, "since I'm still in the driver's seat. It's considered 'standing.' If a cop comes, he'll just tell us to move on."

Emma's heart was in knots, had been since she'd laid eyes on Peter earlier. She looked at him wistfully. *Why did he have to be so wonderful?*

He asked again about her job, but she said, "What about yours? Why are you free to come and drive me to work?"

"I put Sy in charge of a meeting. If I can't do that, what fun is it being the owner and CEO?" He smirked. "Now, tell me what you're walking into when you leave this car."

Emma sighed. Her job was trying. As the newest in the office, though executive secretary for the boss and technically the senior one, she was sure the two other secretaries were taking advantage of her. Almost daily, Emma was given new tasks and paperwork to take over. As soon as she mastered a daily procedure, Linda, a long-time junior secretary, and the worst offender, and would give her a new one. Meanwhile, Linda started putting her feet up on the desk and sipping coffee while Emma's desk had stacks of work to get through.

Her boss shrugged helplessly if Emma pointed out the situation. When Emma asked Linda why she could do nothing all day, she'd say, "Oh, Glenis said I could put my feet up. My blood pressure's high today." Or, "I finished my work for the day. Oh, aren't you done, yet?" Emma would never consider putting her feet up even if she reached "done."

The other women in the office were nurses. They came in between shifts to write their reports and fill other paperwork. She learned from them that Linda was the darling of the bosses and would not be asked to work harder. It was as though she had some strange power over them.

Emma tried not to get bitter about it, but the edge in her voice as she explained this to Peter was unmistakable. He nodded while listening, his eyes thoughtful. His wrist-device dinged but he ignored it.

"Do you hope to stay at this job until you finish school?"

"I guess so. There's a partial tuition reimbursement plan, which I need."

They talked some more but all too soon, she had to leave. With wistful regret she said, "Thank you. You gave me a lovely surprise to start my day. I never expected it!"

"I'll do it again sometime." His wrist phone dinged. He gave a wry grin. "As it is, Sy is having a conniption that I'm not there yet." He checked the time and said, "He should be warding off difficult questions from investors about now, I believe."

She leaned over to give him a quick kiss. Peter met her, took her in his arms and pressed his mouth against hers. His kiss was warm and sweet, firm but not insistent—just like him. When they moved apart, looking into his eyes, she had to brush away a tear.

"Are you upset?" His eyes were troubled.

"I'm fine!" She tried to smile.

"Did I do something wrong?"

She shook her head. "No. It's just the opposite!" She turned to go but stopped before leaving the car. "You do everything right." Quickly she got out of the car and strode off. She felt Peter's eyes following her until she ducked into the parking garage. She'd cross it and use the inside door to the hospital.

Her heart ached. She was falling in love with Peter, she couldn't deny it. She'd tossed and turned the night before weighing the pros and cons of telling him everything, but loving him made the prospect harder, not easier. Knowing Peter was to love him. To love him meant she couldn't risk losing him.

Had she met the pompous businessman Ricky had said she'd be dealing with, even then, it would have been virtually impossible for her to follow the diabolical plan. Everything inside Emma cringed at the thought of having to be intimate with any man, thanks to Loreen's boyfriend Joey, the one who'd abused her. Even with Peter, in her heart Emma knew she didn't want to face what was required of her. She couldn't imagine facing it. Even under such dire circumstances like hers, she did not want to sleep with a man, period. Joey's callous brutality had her scarred for life. Her situation was hopeless from the start—if only she'd told Ricky this at the outset. Maybe he'd have come up with another plan.

She thought about Peter being religious. He'd said every good gift came from God. A desperate plea flew from her. *God, if you're there in heaven, I need your help!*

As she nodded at acquaintances on her way to Utilization—the department where she worked—she suddenly realized that perhaps Peter was heaven's gift, not to make it harder for her but easier. She still needed a settlement, but it didn't have to be a con!

She loved Peter. If he could love her back, she could risk asking him. If he loved her enough, she might not even have to break up with him in order to ask.

It was the first ray of hope in a long time.

When she got in view of the door to her department, she saw two women standing around as if waiting for someone. They turned at the sound of her approaching footsteps and her heart sank. It was Lila and her stepmother, Loreen. "I'm running late," Emma said, as soon as she got close. She had the keys out, as she usually arrived about ten minutes early to open up. Then she'd run down to the cafeteria to get coffees for herself and the boss, Glenis. She liked doing it, as it beat sitting at deskwork.

"You can be a minute later," said Loreen sourly.

Emma stopped. "Fine. What is it?"

Lila said, "You know what it is! It's Peter! I don't know how you got to him," she said in a snarling tone, her eyes like daggers, "but I'm going to let him know all about you."

"What doesn't he know about me?" Emma asked, in an unbelieving tone.

"That you and your dad are cons!"

"That's a lie!" Emma cried.

Glancing at her mother, Lila continued, "Mom's gonna meet with him and set him straight. How your father only married her because she had more money than he did."

"That's not true!" Emma cried. She turned to Loreen. "You knew HE had money! That's why you married him!"

She made a scoffing sound. "He blew his money. But he got hold of mine, all right, and lost all that, too, at the races! He was a no-good bum and you are just like him." She paused, putting her hands on her hips. "We were getting along fine until the two of you came along."

"We lived on Long Island near the beach!" Lila cried.

"Why I listened to your father and moved into Queens, for heaven's sake, I don't know." Her nose wrinkled in distaste. "All he wanted to do was be closer to Belmont to lose his money at the track! I should have known!"

Emma's eyes watered. She missed her father. "Maybe having your boyfriends over during the marriage drove him to it! Such as the one who raped me!" Emma blushed. She'd never said a word about it before to Loreen or Lila and hadn't planned on doing so now.

Loreen's eyes blazed. "What are you talking about? No one I went out with was like that!"

"Joey was! Dad caught him in the act, but it was too late! You weren't home—you were out drinking or something, as usual! So don't give me this garbage about my dad being the low life. If he lost your money, he didn't intend to."

She glanced at Lila and noticed she'd gone pale. And was silent. Emma suddenly realized that Loreen's boyfriend had probably abused her too.

"He didn't intend to? Well, I never intended to get drunk!" Loreen replied hotly.

Emma said. "I have to go. What do you want from me?"

The women eyed her angrily, both with tight lips. Finally, Loreen said, "We want you to stop seeing Peter. Lila still loves him and they only had a misunderstanding. It can be fixed."

Emma stared tragically at Lila, knowing it could not be fixed. "How could you do it?" she asked, almost in a whisper. "Knowing Peter—how could you break up with him?"

"How could I give up his money, is that what you mean?" she snarled.

"I mean, how could you give him up?" She blinked back more tears. "Peter is the sweetest man I have ever met!"

She turned and fumbled with her keys—she was too upset to see straight—but finally got the door unlocked. She went inside and slammed it solidly behind her while her pounding heart filled her ears.

In the hospital corridor, Loreen and Lila looked at each other in surprise.

"The nerve!" said Lila. "She acts like she's got a big heart!"

Loreen drew in a deep breath, her eyes simmering with anger. "We'll see if she has a heart." She turned and walked determinedly toward the elevator to leave. "And if she does— it can be broken."

Chapter Fifteen

During the two bus rides through Flushing from work, Emma could not get her mind off anything except Peter and her predicament. At the apartment, she made a quick vegetable omelet, wondering for the umpteenth time if Ricky was exaggerating when he said they'd kill her and her family if she didn't pay. Would the mob really kill Adam, a young college student with his whole life ahead of him for the sins of his father? Not to mention the rest of her family. And why should she pay for her father's poor judgment, anyway? Why hadn't they gone to Loreen or Lila for that matter? If they'd caught Lila while she was dating Peter, she could have appealed to him for help. She had a clean slate with him at that point. How much easier it would have been for her to get their money!

But it was Emma's burden. It was her job to ask him. She tried to envision how the conversation would go. But no matter how she framed it, it seemed doomed. He'd see through her. He'd find out she'd been after financial help all along—that Ricky had set up the whole situation. It hadn't been her wish, but he'd mark her as a phony, the same as Lila. No, worse than Lila! Because Emma started out complicit, knowingly pursuing a payout. Lila might have fallen in love with his wealth along the way but had probably begun dating Peter because of his charm; he had plenty of it. Emma hadn't even met Peter but had been willing to perpetrate devious purposes. No matter that she'd expected him to be an evil giant, a Goliath, the embodiment of all that could be wrong with capitalism. That was how Ricky had painted him. But all Peter would know was that she was after his money, just like Lila.

If only she could run away from it all… Or, if only she could confess everything to Peter! Could she? It would crush her if he knew the truth but didn't believe her motives. And she'd be as penniless as ever and still in debt to the mob. Four lives were in her hands. She had to see this through, stick to the plan.

Frantically, she thought again about going to the police. She'd thought of doing it a thousand times. But New York cops were notoriously blind to mob activities. "Bought and paid for," Ricky described them. Perhaps the FBI? They might not believe her. And how did one get in touch with the FBI? What was she thinking? Even if they protected her, her brother would be in danger. And Loreen and Lila. Was it likely they'd be able to protect all of them? Did they do witness protection plans for people whose lives were threatened due to a father's failure to repay a debt? Her heart sank lower and lower.

She finished up the dishes just as the phone rang.

"Hey, it's Peter."

"Hello!" She was so glad to hear from him.

He chatted for a few minutes, saying he'd enjoyed seeing her that morning, and was she free on Friday night?

Emma had a class and hated missing even one, as it could mean the difference between getting an A or not. But this wasn't just about her. Lives were at stake. She had to be available. Besides, she wanted to be.

"I can be."

"Great. We'll do something informal this time, okay? Something fun."

"Last time was fun." Lila dumping a glass of water over her came to mind. "Mostly."

He clucked his tongue. "I know. Lila. I still feel bad about that."

"So what will we do?"

"Would you mind meeting my parents? They're back in town for two weeks and asked me to come by."

Emma gulped. He wanted her to meet his parents? Was Peter serious about her? The thought both thrilled and frightened her. "That will make me nervous!" she hedged.

"No, no. They're easy, I promise."

"Like you," she said, and meant it.

She could almost see his boyish grin. "They're planning a light supper on the patio. Nothing fancy. I'll pick you up at 6:00 tomorrow, if that works for you."

"Sure."

"Pack an overnight bag. I mean, to stay the whole weekend, if you can."

Emma's heart constricted. Here it was—he was assuming they'd sleep together.

"You'll have your own room."

Relief flooded her. "Thank you!" she cried, feeling guilty for what she'd thought.

Peter chuckled. "Ah, ah," he said. "I know what you were thinking."

Emma blushed and was glad he couldn't see her. "Well, yes, you had me worried there."

"I have exceptionally good morals," he said. "Ask me why sometime, and we'll talk."

"I will!"

They chatted for a few minutes longer, finalizing plans. Emma couldn't get over how Peter was still behaving in a manner that was too good to be true. Was he for real? What if he was as good a con as she was? It served her right for being so duplicitous—now she felt distrustful of everyone. But Peter had no reason to con her. She had nothing he would need to trick her out of, except, perhaps, sex. But why would he bother when there were no doubt plenty of easy targets?

Overall, his call gave Emma hope—she reveled in knowing she'd be seeing him again so soon, despite the fatal shadow of gloom that was never far off. And now, thank God, she had some good news to give Ricky. He'd love that Peter invited her to his parent's home.

The phone rang again, but it was Lila.

"Now what?" Emma asked.

"You never answered my question. How'd you do it? How'd you get to Peter?"

Emma was tempted to tell her the whole sordid truth, but she would not smear her father's name any further to Lila or Loreen, who already were vicious about him. Besides, if she told Lila, "they" would find out. And who knew what they'd do to them all then?

She decided a hard approach was best. "Look, Lila, you blew it. It's not my fault you're a jerk, okay?"

"You're taking advantage of him!

"You're confusing me with you. I am not you. I like Peter for who he is, not because he's wealthy. He is a great guy!"

"Yeah, sure. You're in it for what you can get. But you can't sleep your way into marriage with him, you know."

"As if I'd want to do that?"

"Why wouldn't you?"

"I just wouldn't! You don't know me, Lila."

Lila was silent. Emma could just see smoke spewing from her ears. Finally, she said, "I know this. Peter is a very religious person. I tried to get religion for his sake, but I never felt it, and honestly, I think it's just a cover. I think he's gay."

"Why?" Emma asked. "I've never had that impression." But suddenly she wondered. Peter was unusually well-behaved for a man when it came to intimacy. He'd said he had "exceptionally good morals," but was it a cover?

"Because he never tried anything. That's like—weird. Or gay."

"He's got really good morals," Emma said, though the words suddenly sounded weak. Not that Lila would know anything about good morals.

"If he's gay, will you still go out with him?

"I—don't know."

"Would you marry him, if he asks you?"

Emma's heart twisted. She hoped Lila was wrong. "I—I don't know."

"If he asks you, marry him, you idiot! Then you can repay my mom for what your dad blew at the tracks."

"Ha! And will your mom return my virginity?" Emma regretted the words as soon as they were out but couldn't retract them. "I'm sorry," she said. "I shouldn't have said that."

"You're no different than I am," Lila said softly. "You're with him because he's rich."

Something snapped and Emma cried, "I'm not like you! I'm falling in love with him, if you must know! How could I not? You know better than anyone what a doll he is. I wish I didn't care so much, but I do! He is the sweetest man I've ever met. I wish life were different and I was free to—" She couldn't say more, but she wished she was free to love him without the mob on her back, free to fall in love without feeling underhanded about it.

"Free to what?" Lila demanded.

"Just free, okay?"

"I don't know what you're talking about."

"No, you don't, so can we please be done here?" She sighed, but with sudden insight, realized that Lila was still in pain over Peter. Her call was about sharing that pain. Suggesting Peter was gay was probably intended to scare Emma, to give her pain too. The bottom line was Lila had lost wonderful, sweet Peter. Emma said sincerely, "Lila—I'm sorry. It must be hard for you—having lost him."

The call ended abruptly.

Emma called Ricky the following day to tell him the news about the weekend.

"Perfetto!" he exclaimed. "Good work."

A tidal wave of guilt crashed over Emma. "I may come clean and just ask for his help."

"No." His voice was firm. "Give him a taste on Friday night and reel him in."

"A taste?"

"Of what he'll get if he puts a ring on your finger. You know what I mean."

Emma hesitated.

"Well?" he asked, annoyed. "Is there a problem?"

"I don't want to hurt him."

"You're worried about hurting the feelings of a billionaire? You ought to be worried about the noose that's gonna go around your pretty little neck if you don't come through. Not to mention the weights that'll put your sweet little brother and stepfamily at the bottom of the Hudson and keep them there."

Bile rose in Emma's throat. "Why didn't your mobsters go to one of them? When Lila was dating Peter, she could've got what they wanted. Why is it all on me?"

"Well…" He paused. "They just caught up with the debt, I guess. And they probably figured you have the best chance of getting it back."

"Why would I have the best chance?" It didn't make sense.

Ricky snorted. "Look, your stepsister is sharp, but you're the best looking."

"That's why it's all on me? That is the stupidest thing I've ever heard!"

"You don't have to like it, princess, you just have to come through with the *denaro.* "

Emma paused, swallowing more bile. He was right. She may not like it but what choice did she have? She choked out, "I'll do the best I can."

"You'll do whatever it takes!" Ricky said in an acid tone.

Friday was four days away, but each day felt interminable. Then, on Thursday during work, Peter called and apologetically told her he'd be tied up until late Friday night. He added, "Since we won't have dinner together tomorrow night, can I come for you on Saturday, say, 8:30? We have a great breakfast planned."

"Sounds like fun," Emma said. She was eager to see him, but it was a relief to have a reprieve until Saturday. Her angst about her situation only intensified when she was with Peter.

After work, she spent hours in the nearest shopping district in search of the right casual outfit for Saturday. Peter said they'd attend church on Sunday, so any of her office ensembles would work for that. But what was the right outfit to hang out with a billionaire's family? Did such a thing exist at her pay grade? The weather was borderline hot and could get worse in May on Long Island, so she chose navy capris and a blue and white striped boat-neck blouse. White hoop earrings and matching necklace, and a blue cottony scarf rounded it off. She bought white fling sandals, mentally settled on the clothing she'd wear for Sunday from her closet, but simply could not find a small thank-you gift. What kind of gift did you get for people who already had everything?

Then, on the street, she saw a candy shop and picked up a dozen chocolate roses in gold foil. It was more than she should spend but seemed like a safe bet. Most people loved chocolate.

When Saturday morning came, after she'd dressed and checked her appearance more than once, Emma was still unnerved. She'd been increasingly uneasy all week, her heart sinking to her shoes at every thought of deceiving Peter. By the time he arrived and gave her a quick peck on the lips at the door, she felt like a bundle of live wires set to explode. At the curb was the limo again—the black one. Rippling with anxiety, she managed a smile as Peter walked her to the car. He shooed off the driver and opened her door himself. He held her elbow while she got in. He was so polite and sweet!

And she was a phony. She wasn't being honest with him. She needed his help, wanted his help, but could not ask for it. She was sunk.

Chapter Sixteen

Peter's parents lived in Old Westbury, Long Island, part of "The Gold Coast" as it was known. After they exchanged small talk in the limo, Peter said, "So…there's something I should tell you before we arrive."

Emma's heart jumped. She was sure it must be something awful. "Yes?"

"Nothing to be alarmed about," he said, reading the feelings on her face. Emma realized he was quite good at understanding her expressions. "It's just that my mother called last night—from Monte Carlo."

"Monte Carlo?" Emma's brows rose.

"She was supposed to fly in last night but she's stuck there for two more days.

She apologized profusely and said she was especially sorry for your sake not to be at the house. She looked forward to meeting you."

Emma swallowed. Peter's mother looked forward to meeting her? "So it'll only be your father?"

"Oh." He shot her a glance, taking his eyes off the road. "No. Um. My dad's there too, with my mom."

"Oh." A wave of relief flicked across her brain. But then caution. "Wait. So it'll only be me and you?"

Peter's mouth creased into a little worry line. "Well, no, us, and a handful of the help."

"The help? They're not my help. They're on your side. That is the same as being alone with you."

He spread his hands. "You're alone with me right now. I'm not dangerous, I promise."

She remembered Sy and Sofia telling her the same thing. And really, she didn't think he was. "I'm sorry. It's a habit to be suspicious of men."

"I don't wonder at it," he said slowly, studying her. She knew he was waiting to see if she was going to elaborate, to tell him how she'd been sexually abused at some point. And maybe at some point, she would. This wasn't the time. Besides, Ricky would be thrilled that they would be virtually alone. It was just the position he wanted her in. "Give him a taste," he'd said. But her heart sank at the thought. Not of spending time with Peter— but at what she was supposed to get from him afterward. Sadness and frustration filled her. The plan would never work. Peter probably went through scads of girlfriends. Girlfriends who were "friendlier" with their natural endowments than Emma, no doubt.

The car turned into the parking lot of a huge mall and Emma realized they were making a stop. She looked at Peter with curiosity. He said, "Just a quick stop."

When the limo came to a halt at the entrance of another Bentsen's Department Store, Emma saw the driver hop out of the car and enter. "So, what're you getting?" she asked, trying to sound casual. She had a suspicion, knowing Peter, that it was something for her, and she wasn't sure she felt good about accepting more gifts from him.

"Well, we never had that dance I promised you."

"Okay. So what are you getting?"

He smiled. "You'll see."

In a minute, the driver returned gingerly carrying a tissue-wrapped item across both his arms. A shopping bag hung from one wrist.

It must be a dress, Emma thought with dismay, judging by the mountain of tissue, not to mention what looked like layers of red taffeta peeking out.

He opened the door and handed the item carefully to Peter, then put the shopping bag on the floor. Peter turned to Emma. "I want to have that dance with you. Since Lila ruined the last gown, I saw this in our catalog and hoped you'd love it."

"She ruined my night but not the dress," Emma said.

"It was dry clean only," Peter said.

He knew his store's clothing, all right. She could still see where the wet spots had been but she planned on taking it to a dry cleaner to see if they could iron out the faint difference in the fabric.

He moved the tissue-wrapped item toward Emma. "Here, take a peek."

Emma gingerly moved aside the layers of tissue and held up the top half of the dress. "It's gorgeous!" It was a strapless deep burgundy red, echoing the thrill of blood in her veins. A matching sash circled the top and would go about her shoulders.

"I didn't even have to think about it. I saw it in a meeting while we went over new arrivals with one of our store buyers. It'll look great on you." He didn't add that it was one of their most expensive gowns, but she cried, "You're spoiling me!"

Leaning toward her, he smiled and kissed her. "I enjoy spoiling you."

Emma flushed, torn between pleasure and discomfort at the same time. "What if it doesn't fit?"

"Do you want to go in and try it in a dressing room? I'll make sure you have help."

Embarrassed at the thought of having help, Emma said, "You were right on the money with the last dress. I think I'll trust your judgment."

"You know what? Try it on right here. I'll get out. There's plenty of room."

She looked past him through the window to see outside, then blinked at him in astonishment.

"The windows are privacy tinted, stronger than most cars. No one can see inside—including me."

She glanced at the dress. "I'll see what I can do."

"Good." He turned to leave.

"Wait." Emma was wearing a back-zip blouse. "Can you open my zipper, please?"

"With pleasure," he said with a wink.

She thanked him afterward, and he left the car, shutting the door firmly behind him. She heard the clicks as all the doors locked, then fingered the copious material of the gown. It felt satiny with an overdress of net or gauze. Call it by any name, it was gorgeous.

While she cautiously removed her top and pants, she mused about this unexpected gift. Peter was his usual generous self, but ought she to accept gifts when she was scheming to ask him for wads of dough later? As much as she enjoyed him and his gifts, she wished she could meet him all over again and know nothing about his wealth. She wished she had met him before learning of her dad's debt. His soft blue eyes, the boyishness of his excitement over little things like popping out of a sunroof to look at the city at night—she loved it. Ricky had never made her smile or laugh very much. And the few guys she'd attempted to date were never gentlemanly like Peter.

While she drew the gown carefully up, she remembered it was strapless and she'd have to take off her bra. In the limo.

It had sturdy bust support, which was reassuring, but she moved as quickly as possible to get into it. Outside, she could see Peter speaking to Jack, the driver, about five feet from the car. Good-looking as ever, his tall, lean frame was a head higher than Jack's. His blond hair rustled in the breeze, and when he smiled as he spoke, she felt warm inside, recalling the effect of that smile when directed her way.

Finished adjusting the gown as best she could, she admired its draping layered skirt. There was no full mirror to be sure, and she couldn't quite stand upright in the car, but it seemed to fit perfectly. All she needed was for Peter to zip up the back. Holding it up with one hand, she knocked on the window.

Peter looked over, then came to the door. She heard the click as it unlocked. He opened it without peeking in. "Ready for me?" he asked.

"Yes."

He leaned in and swept his gaze over her while she held up the gown.

"You look beautiful! I knew you would. But you forgot the shoes." He ducked around her to grab the shopping bag, took out the shoes, and helped her into them in his shoe salesman, confident way.

"They feel great," she said, rocking her feet up and down. But she turned her back to him and asked, "Can you finish zipping me up? To make sure it fits?"

"I sure can," he said, zipping the dress. "But it'll fit. I had you right last time. My time managing the women's clothing department was not in vain. I can pretty much guess any woman's size."

She turned her head to give him a look of mock disapproval. "Poor us!"

"C'mon. Let me see you stand up in it." He motioned to the outside.

Emma flushed but figured she'd never be readier for the public eye than in that dress. He handed her out of the car, and she did a little circle, smiling but very self-conscious.

"I do have good taste if I say so myself." He nodded approvingly.

He waited outside again while Emma changed back into her regular clothes.

"To your parent's house, now?" she asked when he returned.

"The Old Westbury house, yes."

"Is there another?"

He glanced at her as if the question surprised him. "Oh, uh, in Sagaponack. Well, that's mine, but they use it more than I do." He paused. "I live mostly in Manhattan since I work there. But since you asked, we have a place in Monte Carlo, which is where my folks are now. And a couple condos, one in Aspen, one on the Keys, and one in Switzerland."

"You own them all jointly?" It seemed like a surprising arrangement.

"The Westbury and Monte Carlo house are theirs alone, the rest are mine."

About thirty-five minutes later they turned in at an ornate, massive gate. The limo stopped and Jack entered a code that opened it. They moved smoothly forward along a beautiful, winding, tree-lined drive which eventually opened to a wide circle with a sprawling, Old-World-style mansion sitting prominently and impressively in the center. Elegant, manicured landscaping was the perfect complement to the stately dwelling.

"Wow!" she exclaimed.

"It's a relic," Peter said with a wry grin, "built in 1923."

"A relic?" Emma shook her head. "It's gorgeous!"

He smiled. "It's got charm. It's the Tudor Revival Style, inspired by English Gothic country houses." Jack pulled to a stop in front of white-flagged stone steps to the house. The door opened instantly, revealing a man in dark clothes who started down the steps.

Peter leaned toward Emma to say something, but she was distracted by the man who had instantly filled her with alarm.

"Who is that?" As usual, her suspicious brain kicked in with the idea that he was one of the mobsters, that this had all been a setup and Peter was part of them! But he looked past her and said, "That's Nelson. He'll put the car away for us."

Nelson retrieved her suitcase from the trunk and placed it on the front steps. Emma had sudden visions of Lila coming here under just the same circumstances. Perhaps Peter had said she would meet his parents. Perhaps he'd told her the same thing about their being in Monte Carlo.

Surely Lila's wrath wasn't only that she'd lost Peter and his billions, but that she'd given herself to him and still lost them. All her talk about Peter being gay was just to scare Emma.

As if reading her troubled thoughts, Peter said, "Emma." Earnest blue eyes met hers. "Please don't be uncomfortable. I'll keep someone with us at all times if you like. I thought about calling you this morning and canceling the weekend, but I just couldn't." He looked deeply at her. "I didn't want to. I wanted to be with you. And I wanted to bring you here."

Here he was, melting her heart again. What a fool she was, with all her groundless worries. "I'm glad you want to be with me. I want to be with you too. But I do feel uncomfortable..." If only she could tell him why! But she wanted to get one thing straight, and eyed Peter soberly. "I need you to understand that I'm probably not like most girls you date. I'm not open to— um—premarital sex."

She swallowed and waited for his reaction. She expected he'd send Nelson away and turn them back toward Flushing. Ricky would have her head! But she cared for Peter. And, oddly, even if she could put her past bad experience aside, she realized it would be impossible to give herself to him anyway, because he'd be giving himself to her, too. His heart could be on the line. Maybe she was wrong, and it wouldn't mean a thing to him. But what if it did? What if his heart was in it? And if she asked for a settlement, it could be broken. She must not break it.

Peter's brows rose but he smiled. "I remember. You made that pretty clear when we first met. But don't worry—I'm not, either." He winked. "Besides, I don't date a lot. C'mon, let me show you the place."

Emma got out of the car feeling as if she'd been saved from death. She'd thought for sure Peter would be done with her. Was it true he didn't date a lot? Didn't billionaires get what they wanted from women whenever they liked? And if he'd taken her home and been done with her, she really would be in mortal danger. But her relief was tempered by reality—Peter's response was merely a reprieve. She had only bought time. She still had to somehow avoid conning him while getting what she needed. The situation was impossible. But she was saved from failure for now.

While Peter had a few words with Jack at the driver's door, Emma stood waiting, marveling at what he'd said. *I don't date a lot.* Recently he'd said he had good morals, and she should ask him about it. *Strange.* She didn't know what to make of it and feared that Lila was right about him. For her part, it was fear and stubbornness more than morality that kept her clean. Sex was off the menu for survival. No guy would change her mind—now she knew not even a billionaire could, though she was definitely attracted to him. No, not even the mob at her neck could make her cave, though it should because her brother's life was on the line! She didn't want Loreen and Lila to die, either.

But there was no guarantee that giving herself away would save them.

Peter took her suitcase. Emma took a deep breath and headed with him up the steps to the impressive house. He reached for her hand with his free one and gave her a darling smile.

The familiar feeling of happiness mixed with hopelessness swept through her.

From Ricky's perspective, she had today and tomorrow to "work on him," hoping he'd make some sort of commitment. Except she was the one falling in love. Stubborn courage, or maybe it was rebellion, blossomed in her heart like a dormant seed given water—there would be no more waffling or considering it. She simply couldn't follow Ricky's plan. She would not use this time to make him and his mobsters happy. These days were an opportunity to be with the sweetest, best guy she'd ever met. Really, he was adorable. How he'd managed not to snag a wife by now, she couldn't understand. But these days were theirs to enjoy. She might have to face the music afterward—maybe she was being incredibly foolish— but she would enjoy this time with Peter and pretend Ricky didn't exist.

Her father's debt didn't exist. The peril to her family didn't exist.

She had two days to live a fairy-tale life with a billionaire in his luxury castle. Ricky and Peter both had called her 'princess,' so a princess she would be, and Peter was her prince.

For two days.

Chapter Seventeen

As he opened the door to the house, Peter asked, "Are you as hungry as I am?"

Emma nodded. "I'm ready to try this fabulous breakfast if that's what you mean."

He led her outside to a beautiful patio surrounded by manicured landscaping. A table set with a floral centerpiece, crystal and linen napkins, and elegant dishes awaited them. The view included an awesome inground pool and pool house that Peter explained had just been opened for the season. One end of the pool looked like a tropical paradise with a waterfall and palm trees—palm trees on Long Island. Circling the pool on the patio were lounge chairs, sun umbrellas, and a refreshment bar.

"How do those trees stay alive through the winter?" she asked.

"They're taken to the greenhouse."

Nelson and a woman named Marcella served them. Each time one of them came with something, whether coffee, delicate croissants with a yummy-looking filling, an egg and vegetable omelet, fruit salad, bacon or sausage, Peter thanked them very politely, so Emma did too. But she felt as privileged as a princess. She might have been at a super exclusive resort, but to Peter and his family this was normal!

"Do you have all your meals served?" she asked.

"No." He chewed, thinking. "But I do have a chef. I know, it sounds pretentious, but I like healthy food and I don't want to spend time cooking." Marcella appeared with a small tray of hot-from-the-oven pastries, still steaming alluringly, which she placed gently on the table. "Marcella here comes into the city on most Sundays and cooks a week of meals for me." Peter glanced appreciatively at the woman, who smiled in return.

"He's lazy," she said, looking at him with smiling affection.

Peter nudged her playfully. "Good thing for you, or you'd be out of a job." He turned to Emma, "Anyway, I only have to heat them up."

Emma nodded. "That's great!"

"Do you cook?" He looked at her curiously.

"I do, but I like baking more."

"Oh—baking isn't cooking?" he asked, surprised.

Emma smiled. "To me, cooking means meals. Baking is making fun stuff like bread and desserts. Not exactly healthy, but very yummy." After a moment she added, "I'm very good at oatmeal bread."

He nodded. "I like oatmeal bread." Looking at her plate, he said, "Don't eat all of that. I think there's more coming."

She gaped at him. "I'm already full. I don't usually eat breakfast."

"But this is brunch. You eat lunch, right?"

She nodded. "I just ate enough for lunch."

He gave her a mock frown. "I've got today and tomorrow to impress you with sumptuous meals. You have to eat more."

She sat back with a wry smile. "Peter—everything here is impressive. Everything about you is impressive. But you know what impresses me most? You, just being you. You're down to earth and unlike every idea I've ever had about someone so wealthy—if I ever thought about it. I mean, I expected an arrogant, paunchy, crude man."

"You expected?" he asked. "Did you expect to meet me?"

Uh-oh. Emma blushed. She'd made a mistake. "I mean, when I learned about your wealth, it just astonished me that you weren't older and yes, arrogant."

He laughed. "Arrogant, paunchy, crude…that sounds really…low class. You think it takes arrogance and coarseness to make money?"

Emma shrugged. "I don't know about making it, but it seems to follow having it."

He nodded. "Maybe for some. But my parents aren't like that even though the family's been hugely successful." He looked away and back at her. "I hope I'm never like that."

Sincerely Emma said, "I can't imagine you being like that."

While their eyes met, he leaned toward her to take her hand.

She said, "If you don't want women going after you for your money, shouldn't you take the opposite approach? Don't impress me with your wealth.

Show me you need money. Show me you're not going to make my life easier. Aren't you doing exactly the opposite of what you should do?"

His eyes lit with amusement. "I see your point but remember what made us meet. I was there with the sole purpose of dazzling you. And correct me if I'm wrong, but you rejected my every advance when money was all you knew about me."

She smiled gently, remembering. Her aversion to Peter's come-ons, combined with her resolve not to sleep with a man until marriage had worked in her favor with him—who would have thought? Even now, when he might have expected more physical intimacy from her, she'd rebuffed that idea and still he wasn't put off! She almost wanted to pinch herself. Peter seemed too good to be true. But the cloud of worry that Lila had set off descended about her. Perhaps that was the catch. Lila had been right after all.

She ate when the next two courses came, not solely to please Peter but because the food was amazing. "Marcella's wonderful!"

"She brought a lot of her know-how from Colombia. Then my parents sent her to France to learn more."

"Wow." Emma grinned. "She came from Colombia to train in France to cook in an English-style mansion."

"And we're blessed to have her," he said.

She nodded and took a bite of an elegant tartlet, dusted with nutmeg. "I can see why, too. Everything's delicious."

"Tell Marcella. She'll be pleased."

After breakfast, and because it was a beautiful day, Peter took her on a walking tour of the house. In one room, Emma noticed beautiful, sharp photographs of wildlife or nature, framed in simple wood that seemed to set them off more than an elaborate frame might have. When she stopped to admire one, Peter said, "You like it? I took that picture."

She turned to him. "Wow. You're good."

"Was," he said. "I don't have time for that, anymore."

"Never?"

"Sometimes when I'm on vacation I take out my equipment. But not often."

They moved on. Some rooms were elegant, some homey, all tasteful and beautiful. The library was wainscoted and intimate, fitted with sofas and reading spaces meant for comfort. There were many cozy nooks in the house, it seemed to Emma. She wondered if anyone ever used them. In the large kitchen gleaming with stainless steel fixtures and copious counter space, Marcella stood at the stove, stirring something that smelled wonderful. She smiled and nodded at them.

Peter's room was a suite, the bathroom enormous. He'd had that room, he explained, since he was a child. The bath had been redone, and he'd updated the rest with different upholstery and drapes, but for the most part, it was just as it always had been.

Her suitcase was waiting in a guest bedroom with a wonderful old-fashioned canopied bed. An elegant chandelier, rich wallpaper, a beautiful area rug and draperies, along with a polished mahogany dresser, made it feel exactly like what a room for a princess should be—perfect.

The adjoining bath was updated with expensive-looking tile. There was a shower, but also a lovely clawfoot tub with a privacy curtain pulled to one side. Like a posh hotel, every amenity Emma could want was laid out neatly, only not in little travel sizes but full size, and there were thick towels and a plush robe on a hook. It made Emma want to take a bath!

After they'd been through the house, he said, "Let's walk outside. We have great walkways and an overlook." They started for the back, strolling unhurriedly along a cobbled walkway between flower gardens. The walkway ended, but a wooded trail opened up and they took it. Peter held her hand and told her more about the history of the property. He pointed out his favorite landmarks, such as the little bower of bushes he'd hidden in after his mother said he'd have to go to bed hungry.

"What did you do to earn that?" she asked.

He nodded, remembering. "I scolded Marcella for not making me the dinner I asked for."

"That's it?"

He grinned. "I used a bad word. We weren't allowed to."

"What was it you wanted that she didn't make?" She expected him to name some exotic dish.

"Pancakes." She chuckled while a boyish smile crossed his face.

They stopped at a gazebo on the highest point of the property and looked over the expanse of treetops of Old Westbury. Peter turned to her, "Do you enjoy walking? There's a nice beach we could stroll just a short drive from here."

"Sure," she said. "But aren't the beaches mostly private out here?"

He nodded. "Yes, but I have friends. We can use the beach. I return the favor in Sagaponack if they're out that way."

"You have oceanfront property?"

He gave a wry grin. "For now. I'll be selling it." He paused. "Turns out, I'm not that crazy about the ocean."

Emma nodded. "I like water, but I don't like sand. And not too much sun, either."

Peter lifted her hand and kissed it. "Same here."

In yet another car a few minutes later, a Bentley luxury sedan, he said, "Let's skip the sand. I know a great overlook of the bay. It's private, but we can go."

About fifteen minutes later they got out of the car to admire the bay with the Sound in the distance, all gloriously blue and dotted with bouncing splashes of sun stretching out to the horizon. Connecticut could faintly be made out across the water as a foggy grey outcropping. The masts and sails of distant boats could be seen here or there, moving slowly but peacefully. The coastline, jagged and dotted, stretched in both directions. Emma tried not to think of how it led west to the East River around Manhattan, and then to the Hudson. The Hudson awaiting her and her family if she didn't get a hundred grand from Peter! No, she needed to forget all that and just be present with him in the here and now. She'd promised herself to do that.

They sat on a wall of stone facing the bay, breezes tugging at their hair, and talked. Emma asked lots of questions about Peter's upbringing, still convinced his life must have been like a fairy tale, being so rich. But, as he had told her that first day in his limousine, he was put to work at a young age, and worked hard. If the staff—they didn't call them servants—did anything for him, he was taught to thank them, and mean it. He and his younger brother had to clean up for themselves and weren't allowed to get lazy.

"Oh, and we went to church every Sunday," he said. Then, with a sideways look at Emma, added, "I still do, every week—unless I'm away for business, but even then, I'll watch a service online if I can. I'm also involved in a men's study group." He paused. "You said you don't go to church?"

Emma frowned. "I know I should go. My parents only went occasionally on Easter and Christmas, and Loreen didn't go at all. Dad stopped going after they married." She paused.

"I guess officially I'm a Lutheran, but I've never thought a whole lot about it."

He nodded. "We'll go together tomorrow. I told you that, right?"

She shook her head with a little smile. "You did. I brought an office outfit."

He waved a hand. "That's fine. Church is pretty casual." Soberly he added, "After the service, we'll talk more about this—about God—it's important to me."

Surprised at his serious tone, Emma nodded. "Sure."

He took her for a drive to see the neighborhood and catch more glimpses of the shoreline. Afterward, stopping only for coffee to go, they returned to the car and then the house. Meandering around the property, stopping on a bench here or there, they continued talking and laughing. Emma couldn't tell how much time went by. And watching him as he spoke, she couldn't get over how handsome Peter looked. She'd always thought him good-looking, but now he was beautiful! How could someone's appearance change like that? And she was loving every second of their time together. Now and then the dark shadow of her mission threatened to rear its ugly head, but each time, she quashed it down to give Peter her full attention.

They took some more turns and detours—he knew every inch of the property—but stopped short of exploring the front grounds, as he felt they'd done enough walking for one day. Recalling the long, wooded drive from the street, Emma was glad.

They came to a one-story wing of the house with steps leading to a veranda on the roof. He led the way up and they took seats side-by-side that gave a different view of the back.

"How pretty," she said. "Your parents don't mind that we're using their house?"

"They love it. They travel a lot so they encourage me to bring friends. But you know, that's one hazard we face"—he shot her a rueful look— "finding genuine friendship. Everybody loves the rich guy. That's what my dad says."

Emma nodded. "I'm sure that's true, but it's not much easier for the rest of us."

He met her eyes looking thoughtful. "Really?"

"Really. Genuine friendship is rare no matter who you are. I have one best friend, Nadia Haseltine. And her boyfriend Chris. They are my dearest and only close friends. Other than them, I have acquaintances."

He paused. "And you're not friendly with Lila and your stepmother."

She almost snorted. "Let's put it this way: they have never been friendly to me. They hate the memory of my father and they don't even know—" She fell silent.

"What don't they know?" Peter asked gently.

Emma swallowed. "They don't know how deeply troubled he was, or the trouble he got himself into."

"What sort of trouble?"

Uh-oh. Emma was getting precariously close to revealing what she must *not* reveal. "Unlike you and your family, he had no financial sense. He died with debt."

Peter nodded. "Hmm. I'm sorry. That must have been hard on all of you."

Tears popped unexpectedly into her eyes, so she looked away. When she'd conquered them, she said, "I only found out about it recently. He kept it really hidden." Her tone was soft but sad.

He cleared his throat. "So Loreen was held responsible?"

Emma turned to him with tormented eyes. *If only that were true!* Frantically, she thought, *Tell him. Tell him now! Tell him I have to repay it!* But fear overcame the urge. He would smell hunger for money and that would seal her fate. He'd be done with her. That she did not allow sexual intimacy, he'd accepted. Against all odds, he'd accepted it. But that she wanted money? That was another thing entirely. He'd pursued her precisely because she'd behaved as though she did not want his money. She couldn't ruin it now. All she said was, "They hate me even more because of it."

"Why? It wasn't your fault."

"I know."

A sliding door behind them opened, and Marcella came out carrying a tray with cold drinks. She served Emma first, saying, "Iced caramel latte." Emma thanked her.

"My favorite! Thanks, Marcella," said Peter.

"You're very welcome," she said with a smile, and then left.

After they sipped their drinks, he said, "Tell me more about your life with Lila and Loreen. I can't remember them ever mentioning you. Not even a mention!"

She sniffed. "I'm not surprised. They never included me in anything. They still wish I didn't exist!"

"Why do you think that is?"

Emma shook her head. "When my dad first married Loreen, I wasn't happy about it. I missed my mother… Loreen never forgave me for not welcoming her and Lila with open arms, I guess." She paused. "We developed this sort of tug-of-war for my father's affections, and he did show favoritism to me. I think he did because I'd lost my mother and Loreen was so cold." She turned injured eyes to him. "Anyway, Loreen cheated on him—she even brought her horrible boyfriends to the house—and things got worse, and my dad was broke, and when he died, they made it clear they wanted nothing to do with me. He died my last year of high school, and I moved out right after graduation."

He squeezed her hand. "You've had it tough." He paused. "What about your younger brother?"

She nodded. "Adam. He was young, and they took care of him. He never experienced being an outcast like I did, but as he got older, it bothered him, the way they treated me. He started making a fuss about it, and when they didn't change, he got angry. When he distanced himself and all but stopped talking to them, of course they blamed me."

He shook his head. "I'm so sorry." He looked at her with such compassion that Emma thought of the rape and whether to tell him. But it was painful to talk about, and she didn't want to come across as a complete wreck with a totally sordid past.

Not to mention, if he really had what he called "exceptional morals," would he look down on her for not being a virgin?

He pulled on her hand, making Emma look at him expectantly. He motioned with his head and patted his lap. "Come here, sit with me."

She smiled and rose.

Situated comfortably on Peter's lap, their eyes met and he kissed her. He kissed her as if he were willing away the pain of her past. "Tonight," he said, in a low, soothing tone, "you're going to forget about all that. Tonight, you're my princess. I have a special evening prepared."

A ripple of pleasure shot through her. Hearing Peter call her his princess felt so completely different than when Ricky used the term!

She grinned. "A special evening? That sounds mysteriously intriguing. But honestly, I feel like every minute with you is—" And suddenly she couldn't speak. She swallowed.

Peter drew her up closer in his arms. "Is what? What were you going to say?"

Emma swallowed the choked-up feeling inside but decided to speak her mind. "That every minute with you is special. You don't need to prepare anything to make it feel that way. It already is."

His mouth twisted between a smile and a frown. "You don't have to sound so tragic about it." He stroked her face. "What's wrong?"

She blinked back the tears. There was no way she would ruin this by letting him know. Instead, she asked, trying to smile, "Which fairy tale? Which princess will I be?"

He shrugged, smiling back. "Take your pick. Wait, don't.

You'll be Princess Emma." He kissed her again. "I like the sound of that."

Despite the cold drink, and that she had showered that morning, Emma felt in need of another shower after all the walking they did. Actually, the thought of that clawfoot tub was awfully appealing, too.

"Of course," Peter said. "Take your time. I have phone calls to make anyway."

He kissed her gently on the mouth, but it turned into a heartfelt kiss. Emma threw her arms around his neck and Peter welcomed her but then suddenly drew back and released her. Looking into her eyes, he said, "I'll see you around seven? Feel free to look around or go wherever you like. The house and grounds are yours. And you'll have time to relax and get changed before dinner and our dance."

Her eyes widened. "Are we going somewhere for this?"

He grinned. "To a ballroom."

"Where?"

"Right here." His smile broadened. "We have a ballroom. It's for parties."

She laughed. "Of course you do. But you didn't show it to me."

"I was going to surprise you. It'll be a ball for two."

Chapter Eighteen

THE CINDERELLA
NIGHT, PART ONE

A phone call had Peter's attention for the next few minutes, but he walked Emma to her guest bedroom and opened the door for her while he spoke. He put the phone aside to give her a kiss on the cheek and whisper, "See you later!"

She shut the door and flopped onto the bed to ruminate and worry. She was well practiced in doing both but never had she had more reason to. A part of her regretted that she hadn't come clean about everything, but another part told her she was exactly right not to. After worrying in earnest for a few minutes longer she realized she could go on stressing forever. Or take that bath.

Minutes later, she sat luxuriating in a bubble bath in the clawfoot tub.

She put her head back on a rolled towel and let the warm water melt away her worries. She imagined living there and taking bubble baths at any time. A large soap bubble floated before her and suddenly Peter's cute grin and blue eyes appeared in her mind. She'd loved every moment with him, but something about that last kiss bothered her. She'd thrown her arms about him, and he'd tightened the kiss, but then abruptly ended it. The soap bubble popped.

She hated to believe it, but it did seem that Lila was right about him being gay. Weren't a lot of super-wealthy people known for "alternate lifestyles?" She'd managed not to think about Ricky and the burden upon her. But even the bubble bath couldn't erase this growing worry.

After washing her hair and drying off, Emma wrapped herself in the thick, cozy bathrobe and went back to rest on the bed. She checked her nails. Good. No chips. She checked her phone and found two messages from Ricky wanting updates. She ignored them. There were five messages from Nadia, all asking a different question about Emma's day. Was it going well? Was she having fun? Was Peter being wonderful? What were they doing? She assured Emma that she and Chris were rooting for her! And they'd looked up where the Bentsen's lived and were going to drive by. That made Emma smile. She texted, "You won't see much. The drive past the gate is about a half mile long—at least." Two seconds later, Nadia called.

"I'm dying! How's it going?" she asked.

"It's going great but I'm dying, not you. At least, I will be."

"What do you mean?"

Emma blinked back tears. "I love him. And the more I love him, the more I can't tell him."

"That's just you being negative!" Nadia said. "Chris, isn't she just being negative?"

Emma heard his reply. "Yeah." She wondered if he would dare say no. "I'm not. I told you about Lila. I can't be another Lila! I won't make him despise me!"

There was some commotion on the other end. Nadia said, "I'm sorry, girl, my mom just dropped in. She won't stay long. I'll call you back."

"Don't. We're having dinner soon."

"Ooh, fun! But OK… How can we help you?" Emma could picture her friend's earnest gaze.

"I don't know. Pray!" *Where had that come from*?

"Pray? Uh—okay! I will and Chris will, too. Right, Chris?"

Before he could answer, Nadia's mother said loudly, "Well, if you're gonna pray, I'll pray too! What are we praying for?"

"Emma," Nadia answered. Into the phone, she added, "Mom's Catholic. We'll go to Saturday mass with her and light candles for you."

"Oh." Emma didn't know Catholics did that. "Does that do anything?"

"I don't know. But it can't hurt, right?" She pictured Nadia smiling and shrugging.

Emma's brows knit. "Don't give her any details, Naddie!"

"I won't. Love ya, girl."

"Love you, too!"

Emma was gowned and ready by ten of six. Studying herself in the mirror, she marveled at how the gown fit her to a tee. Peter was a man who could dress a woman to perfection. She'd guess that Peter would find the right clothing for a woman in any price range.

The shopping bag with shoes also contained another pair of silky-smooth stockings and a little glittery evening purse. That man thought of everything! She put only her phone, lipstick, and her little round makeup mirror inside the purse. She felt she didn't need the purse, but since he'd bought it, she wanted to use it. Besides, she hadn't taken a single picture yet. Maybe tonight she'd have a chance.

She headed to the stairs. At the turn in the landing, she saw Peter at the bottom, dressed to the nines, awaiting her. He watched her coming down with an admiring smile and took her hand and kissed it when she reached him. "Princess Emma," he murmured with a little smile.

They went on to the dining room to one end of the table set romantically for two with candlelight.

A lustrous red rose rested on both plates. The drapes were closed so the rest of the room was darkened, giving the corner a feeling of intimacy.

Peter picked the rose from her plate and handed it to her. Emma thanked him and sniffed it, letting the soft petals caress her skin. She'd thought roses only smelled good on the bush, but the aroma from this one was deeply perfumed. Luscious. Peter broke the stem off his and placed it in the lapel of his dark jacket.

Marcella and Nelson served them as at breakfast, except both were dressed in uniform now. By the place settings and utensils, Emma saw it would be a multi-course dinner. Nerves fluttered in her stomach. Everything was so formal, it made Peter seem further away, for he was used to such surroundings, such a life, but not Emma. She was ordinary.

"You're quiet," he said as if reading her mind.

"I'm…taking it all in."

Peter smiled. "You like it? I told Marcella to make it romantic." He winked.

Emma nodded. "It's beautiful, thank you." Everything Peter touched was beautiful, she thought, even herself in this fairy-tale dress. From the day she'd met him, it was as though an extravagantly soul-stirring symphony had begun playing in the background of her life. Here, right now, it came to the forefront, loud and heart-wrenching, so picture-perfect it was ridiculous—how could it all be real?

Marcella brought in appetizers and a bottle of white wine. Peter prayed for the meal as he had last time, and again, to her astonishment, included a little prayer of thanks for Emma being with him.

Afterward, he said, "Earlier I prayed that you would be able to speak to me about whatever's on your mind."

Emma's eyes widened. "Excuse me?" Her throat constricted. He'd actually prayed about her? And he knew that something was on her mind?

Studying her, Peter's brows creased. He reached across the table to take her hand. "I haven't wanted to say anything…I thought you needed time. And maybe you do—maybe you need more time before you tell me. But I get the feeling, every time I'm with you, that something is bothering you very much. If I'm doing something wrong, tell me, Emma."

"No! You're not!" She gave him an earnest look, but in seconds she was blinking back tears.

Peter's eyes widened. "See? There it is! You're practically crying. What is it?"

Emma looked away. This beautiful world was crashing in. Her chance to know and love Peter was disappearing. The symphony of her perfect time with him was going to end in a crescendo of discordant notes. She'd been right to feel it was too good to last. All she had to do was tell him the truth and it would end in a cacophony of disillusionment, hurt, and anger.

She swallowed and looked back at him. "You're very perceptive. But it's not you…" She bit her lip. "It's nothing we need to talk about tonight." He looked ready to argue so she hurriedly added, "Can we just enjoy dinner together? I would like to just enjoy being with you. Is that okay?"

His eyes softened, and he sat back, still studying her. Reluctantly he said, "If that's what you want."

She smiled gratefully.

The next hour flew by. When Marcella began clearing the last dishes, Peter thanked her and added, "Tell Nelson I said now." Emma wondered what that was about, but since Peter didn't offer an explanation, she didn't ask. He stood and came and helped her from her chair. She looked up into the intent gaze on the face she loved. He said, "May I have this dance?"

She smiled. "Of course."

He put a hand against her back and led her from the room. "Let's talk tonight. We can talk while we dance, or before we dance, or afterward. But I want to get inside your head. I need to know what's bothering you."

Emma's heart constricted. She wanted to forget all her troubles. Let this weekend be forever a time to remember as only sweet and wonderful. It wasn't the time to come clean and see it all get bulldozed. She tried to think of a way to gracefully get out of talking. The words wouldn't come.

They walked down a short set of wide, marble stairs, and entered a dark area that took only seconds to blink awake with lights that came on in a succeeding fashion until the whole area was lit up. The ballroom. A huge, glittering ballroom, in a private home!

Nelson entered from a far end that led outside. Peter told her to please wait a moment while he went and spoke to him briefly. Afterward, the man strode quickly to the side of the room and disappeared through a door that seemed to lead into a press box. No, it was a sound box, like for a DJ. A minute later, music erupted around them, a beautiful symphonic arrangement she didn't recognize.

It was their symphony come to life! The one that had peeked out at her since she'd met Peter, the one that had tried to play louder only she had stopped it. She had refused to confide in Peter. It was loud and clear now. Peter took her hand and pulled her close. They began dancing. *She must not stop the music.*

This was her weekend to enjoy Peter as if she were free. He wanted to talk, but she must steer him away from the truth.

Having had no dance lessons, Emma felt utterly gauche, but Peter led her gently and easily, just as he'd promised. He drew her closer, holding one hand in his, and kept their pace steady and slow. It felt infinitely sweet to be in his arms. As the minutes passed, the strength of the music, beautiful and romantic, made her free her hand so she could wrap them about his neck.

It wasn't just music but the whole package: Peter, kind, thoughtful, caring; the dress, the shoes, the ballroom. A *Cinderella night.* If she wasn't careful, she'd have to drop her mask instead of a shoe and run home. Peter would find out she was the very thing he wanted to avoid in a woman. *But not tonight. Let it not be tonight!*

After the dance, he looked deeply into her eyes. He hadn't made a move on her, hadn't even tried to kiss her, but she felt it coming now. To her surprise, instead of kissing her he said, "Come with me." He waved at Nelson in the box and then led her by the hand from the ballroom. They went toward French doors leading to a veranda, but still holding her hand, Peter passed them and continued to another set of marble steps across the room, the one Nelson had come through. It led outdoors.

She thought they'd find a nice spot on the patio, perhaps, or return to the house via a different entrance, but Peter led her along the cobblestone path they'd explored earlier. He turned her onto a little side trail she hadn't noticed before but then came to a stop. Emma looked at him expectantly, and he motioned ahead, into a wooded area.

Emma looked and gasped. Ahead of her was a sight that, if nothing else about the night had seemed like a fairytale, this alone would have done it. Ahead of them, in a bower of moonlight and an opening of trees, was a candle-lit oasis. Dozens of flickering candles beckoned them on like a welcoming door to heaven.

The bushes too, sparkled with softly glimmering lights like a million fireflies.

She turned to Peter in awe. "It's like a fairy tale. Now you're really making me feel like a princess!"

He smiled. "I'm glad you like it."

Emma lifted her voluminous skirts to hurry toward the lights. "Like it? It's a dream!"

When she drew closer, she saw the lights were centered around a stone outcropping where they could sit. Peter said, "Let me take your picture." He motioned at a wide, clean rock, so she complied, sitting and arranging her skirts around her. Peter stepped back far enough to get all of her in the shot, as well as some background. She smiled for a few shots, but he kept taking pictures, moving about to get her at different angles.

"You rarely capture people for who they really are," he said, while moving to another vantage point, "in the first few shots. You need to keep at it. Get them off guard. The real person begins to show up."

Alarm filled her heart. Was Peter saying he suspected her of being other than what she was showing him? He would be right, of course. She tried smiling, tried to think happy thoughts.

"Turn away but look back at me over your shoulder."

She did as he asked.

"Put a hand on the shoulder nearest me."

"Are you sure you're not a professional photographer?" she asked, placing her hand across one shoulder. She kept her voice light but felt increasingly unsettled that the real her WAS going to show. The uncertain but scheming girl she had to be in order to survive.

"I'm using my cellphone," he said. "The camera's great, but a professional would use a quality camera." He took a few shots, and she rose.

"That's enough! Let me take some of you."

He came toward her. "I have enough photos of me, but let's do a selfie of us together." He put one arm around her and held out the camera for the shot. Afterward, he tucked it into a jacket pocket.

"Wait," Emma said. "Let's get one with my phone too."

After only one picture, he said, "That's good. I'll send you some of mine." He took her hand and led her to an edge of the candlelit scene where they settled into a deep-cushioned double swing, right there in the woods. Peter put an arm about Emma and drew her close. She rested her head on his shoulder.

Earlier, he'd gazed at her as if she was everything he wanted. She hoped he was not going to raise the subject again of what was bothering her. How differently would he see her if he found out? If he knew she wanted money from him, had wanted it all along—and not a few bucks, either, but a hundred grand!—would he look at her the same way with those beautiful blue eyes?

He shifted to face her so Emma raised her head.

"You don't look happy," he said. "There's something on your mind—it's there often—I'd like to know what it is."

Emma was speechless. Thinking quickly, she said, "You're going all out for me. But what am I doing for you? Nothing! What do I have to offer you? I wish you weren't so…rich!" She meant it, too. If he couldn't help her, their relationship would have been easier and on the level. Yet, if he wasn't rich, they wouldn't have met. She sighed.

He kissed her softly on the mouth. "I'm sorry it makes you uncomfortable, but I'm kinda glad I've got money. And as for what you have to offer? You're being you. You're genuine, and sweet; you're beautiful and kind." He remembered the letters to charity at her apartment. "And generous. That's more than enough."

Emma slumped her head back on his shoulder. Genuine? Sure. Like fool's gold! She was no better to Peter than Ricky had been to her.

Chapter Nineteen

THE CINDERELLA
NIGHT, PART 2

Peter looked at her thoughtfully. "You know what? I'm gonna get us a drink. Do you have a preference?"

"Wine?" Emma thought it would help calm her nerves.

"Sure. Just one." He winked. He kissed her again softly on the mouth. Emma's heart swelled. She threw her arms about his neck and they kissed in earnest, but just like what had happened last time, Peter gently ended the kiss, removing her arms. He came to his feet. "I'll get those drinks. Be right back."

She nodded, but with the little niggling feeling that Lila had been right that he was gay. He had to be. But as she watched him walking toward the house, her heart filled with love. Oh my gosh, she really loved him. No matter what. She loved him so hard it hurt. Looking around, she felt as if she were enveloped in a safe, magic bubble. This was her life, now. She had a man who loved her and whom she loved. Her troubles felt suddenly lighter. She would find another way to repay that debt and tell Peter only after it was done. She didn't have to ruin her relationship with him or destroy this magical, Cinderella night.

She stood and spun in a circle, enjoying the way her long gown filled out. She took a picture of the lights so she could remember this night forever. While still holding the phone, it buzzed and vibrated. Ricky! Couldn't that man leave her alone?

"I asked you not to call me!" she said, looking to make sure Peter wasn't back.

"I had to, princess. Listen! You're out of time! They're tired of waiting. You have to make your move tonight."

"I can't!"

"I don't care if you have to get on your knees and kiss his feet, you gotta ask tonight. They know where your brother is. He's gonna be first. Just sayin'."

Emma's eyes filled with tears. "I can't, not tonight, Ricky," she said, pleadingly. "Trust me. I'm getting close, but this isn't the time."

"I told them that, *sorella*, but it's not good enough. It's tonight or bust."

"Just one more day! I'm that close," she lied.

Silence.

"Ricky, please— this is your fault, you didn't give me enough time!"

"You do this tonight, or it's over for you and your family."

He was gone. The magic bubble burst. Emma was suddenly, brutally, back to reality.

And this was the cold, hard truth. She was in love with Peter Bentsen but had to ask him for a hundred grand. He'd know she needed it all along. He'd know she was a con. He'd know and no longer love her.

As she fought tears, she realized it would have been better for him if he had never met her. Better for him if she disappeared, leaving him with good memories. And suddenly, yes, that was it! She had to disappear. She wasn't Princess Emma, she was Cinderella, and her clock had struck midnight. It would hurt Peter. But that wasn't as bad as hurting him by showing her true colors. He'd hate her, then. He'd shut her out, just as he'd shut out Lila. It was selfish, but she'd rather leave him missing and wanting her. She'd rather leave him in the dark as to what happened than let him see who she really was. She called Nadia.

"Em! Yes! I'm dying to know how it's going!"

"You and Chris need to come for me. Now!" Her voice shook with emotion.

Nadia hesitated. "Did he try to get you in bed?"

"No! I can't explain. I'll tell you when you get me."

Nadia said, "Okay, okay, lucky for you, we decided to see if we could check out the place, so we drove by. We couldn't see the house so we kept going but we're not too far." Emma heard her ask Chris, "How long til we can be back there?" Louder she said, "We'll be there in about twelve to fifteen minutes."

"I'm heading to the front of the property now," Emma said.

She hurried in that direction. "I think it's more than half a mile, but I should be there by the time you arrive."

"Okay." Nadia sounded subdued. "Are you sure you should do this?"

Emma stifled a sob. "I have to." She paused. "If you don't see me, don't turn into the drive, there's a gate. Just wait at the road, okay? I'll be there."

Nadia sighed. "I hope you know what you're doing."

Emma stashed the phone into her purse, lifted her skirts and hurried her pace. She couldn't move fast with her heels, so she stopped to slip them off. Seconds later, she heard Peter calling her and broke into a panicked run, shoes in one hand, and skirt off the ground with the other. Poor Peter! If only she'd had the courage to tell him! She ought to have given him that chance—but even now, her feet kept moving, her heart still convinced she was doing what she had to. Hot tears fell as she ran, some landing on her legs and feet. She was a fool, a fool! Her phone buzzed. She stopped in case it was Nadia, but it was a text from Peter.

Where are you?

What could she say? She stashed the phone back in the evening purse and kept running. The drive seemed endless! Again, her phone buzzed. This time, Peter was calling.

She swallowed and kept running while more hot tears fell. She needed a tissue! Another ding came and she stopped to check it. *Where are you? You're worrying me.*

She sniffed and swiped her nose with her arm. She had to answer. *I'm fine. I'm sorry, Peter. Just let me go.* She sent it but then wrote one more quick text. *I love you!*

She continued running. If Peter had thought she was a normal human being he was now relieved of that illusion.

She was nuts and now he knew it. For her own sake, she ought to have done what Ricky wanted, only she'd have explained the situation to Peter and then asked for the money.

But he'd despise her! So instead, she was leaving the love of her life, was still in danger from the mob and farther than ever from paying their price. But she'd told Ricky she needed one more day. Now she counted on them giving it to her. What was one more day for them? Nothing. For her, it would buy enough time to warn Adam, Lila and Loreen. Enough time, she hoped, to devise some other way out of the nightmare.

The revving of an engine approaching fast from the house sent a tremor of panic through her. Peter mustn't find her! She scurried off the driveway and ran into the trees lining it. Her heart about stopped when the car slowed down not far from where she was crouched in the brush. Peter's voice, "Emma? Emma! C'mon, we need to talk!"

Her heart burned. How she so wanted to talk! But the very thought of his disgust, his anger, his change of heart toward her, kept her silent. When the car slowly passed, she continued to hear him calling. Tears fell harder. Her head pounded. She was a total loser! Doing this to the sweetest guy in the world!

She finally saw the gate ahead with Peter's car before it. It swung open and he went through, stopped at the road, and then turned right—the direction Emma would go if she was heading home. Emma cautiously went as far as the gate, which had already closed.

There was no sign of Nadia and Chris, or Peter. She waited, her heart hammering.

Minutes later, when her friends pulled over out front, she hurried and pressed the button to open the gate—thank God she didn't need a code to exit. As she went through, she saw Peter's car coming back! She dropped her skirts and ran to the car.

As she fumbled to open the door, Peter pulled alongside in the other lane and stopped.

Looking with great concern at Emma, he hurried from the driver's seat, but she threw herself into the car, pulled the door shut and locked it. "Hurry! Go!" she cried.

Peter was at her door. "Emma!"

"GO, GO!"

Chris stepped on the gas. She turned and gave Peter a look of utter despair. She saw he was confused and hurt. More tears wracked her, and she sobbed. Nadia turned to give her a sympathetic look. Her eyes widened and she grabbed a few tissues from her purse and gave them to Emma. "Are you okay?"

Chris said in a pained voice, "Why don't you let us take you back?"

"No," Emma sobbed. "I can't!"

"He wanted you," Nadia said, turning again to look at Emma, her voice reproachful. "He looked very upset." Her face scrunched into a frown. "Why'd you run? Why?"

Emma buried her face in her hands. "Ricky called and said I had to get the money tonight." She paused and looked up with agonized eyes. "I couldn't do it! I couldn't ask him. And I couldn't go along anymore as if I wasn't after something when I am, because I love him!"

Nadia said, "That is exactly why you should have stayed." In a flat voice she asked, "Where are we taking you?"

"To Adam's dorm."

"In that dress?"

"If I stop at home, Peter could be there."

Nadia turned to Chris. "Go to my place."

Emma cried, "No, that would put you and Chris in danger! My brother is already a target. Take me there."

"Emma, I love you, but that's like four hours away. You can't go in that dress anyway." To Chris, she said, "My place." To Emma she added, "I'll find you some normal clothes."

"No," Emma said. "Just go to Adam's dorm. I can find clothes later."

Nadia turned again. "No, Em. You'll be easy pickings in that."

"They don't know I'm wearing this." She went to put her red pumps back on so at least she'd not be barefoot but found she only had one. The other must have fallen during her run.

When Emma drove off with her friends, Peter was ready to dash back to his car and follow them, but he saw one of Emma's red shoes and bent to get it. She'd dropped it in her hurry to get away. Get away! From him. He was hurt and bewildered. He had no idea what made her run, whether he had said or done anything wrong—well, he must have done something she didn't like, but he hadn't a clue as to what. As he turned the shoe in his hand, his hurt turned to anger. Why couldn't she have told him the problem? Why hadn't she talked about it? Instead of following, he'd look up her friends and pay them a visit. He had a near photogenic memory that worked whether he saw something or heard it. Emma had said, *I have one best friend, Nadia Haseltine.*

He pocketed the shoe and returned to the house. He got online and in less than ten minutes had what he needed. His plan was to wait until the following day, give it some time, but he was restless. He thought about Emma's face as they drove off, tear-stained, agonized. He thought of the text she'd written, *I love you!* Suddenly he was on his way out. This couldn't wait.

Chapter Twenty

When they reached Nadia's apartment, Emma was still crying softly. She'd not only hurt Peter, but she'd lost him. And now she and her family would be wiped out by the mob! None of them had done anything to deserve it, but they were going to lose their lives because of her father's sins. And because she was a coward.

For the first time, she felt hot anger toward her dad. She'd been so busy defending him to Loreen and Lila that she hadn't really stopped to consider if their complaints had validity. And she'd been blaming Ricky for the mess with the mob when in fact it was all her father's fault! He must have known what would happen.

Why hadn't he warned them? Why had he allowed himself to get in so deep in the first place? Suddenly she felt doubly bereft. She'd lost Peter and she'd lost respect for Dad. She looked up to find Nadia and Chris studying her from the front seat.

"I'm sorry. I was lost in thought."

Nadia nodded. "I know." She and Chris exchanged a look. "C'mon, let's get you dressed in something that isn't attention-getting."

Emma peered outside. "I wanted to go to Adam's dorm."

"You're not thinking clearly," Nadia said.

"I'm thinking clear enough to know that you're skinnier than I am and your clothes won't fit." She got out of the car.

"We'll find something," Nadia said. Her eyes dropped to Emma's feet. "You're barefoot!"

Emma held up the single red pump. "I lost a shoe while I was running."

"Too bad, great shoes," Nadia said. They entered the building and took an elevator to her apartment on the 4th floor. Nadia turned to Emma with the look of an epiphany.

"What?" Emma asked.

She smiled. "You lost your shoe running! Like Cinderella!"

Emma closed her eyes. "I know. I don't see what's funny about it."

They reached the apartment. Motioning her inside, Nadia said, "It's just funny. You're dressed for a ball, you danced in a ballroom, and you ran from it. Like Cinderella."

Emma plopped on the couch. "Not exactly." She was exhausted. Nadia surveyed her while Chris went to the kitchen for something to drink. She put her hands on her hips. "Why don't you stay the night? We're safe. Chris said the earliest they'll look for you is late tomorrow."

Emma nodded, thinking it over. "Maybe you're right."

"I'm right. You're staying."

They found clothing that fit well enough—nothing to win a beauty contest with, but what did it matter? What did anything matter? In a day or two, she'd be under the Hudson. She almost welcomed the thought.

"You can have my bed," Nadia said. "It's more comfortable than the couch."

"No, thanks," Emma said. "I may not make it through the night."

Nadia frowned. "Like what, are you gonna leave and walk to your apartment in the middle of the night?"

"No." She sighed. "I don't have my keys. They're in the guest bedroom in Old Westbury. But I might call a cab to take me to the college."

Nadia frowned. "Oh, right, because Adam will be thrilled to have you wake him up at 5 a.m. to let him know he's about to die."

"Well, he is!" Emma frowned. "But I left my money and credit card there too! Can you loan me enough?"

"No way. You're staying here." She studied Emma. "You couldn't afford a cab to Cornell, you know. You really aren't thinking clearly. Go to my bedroom and go to sleep."

"Where will you sleep?"

"Right here." She patted the sofa. "But I'll stay up with Chris for a while."

"I should sleep on the sofa."

"I'm not taking Chris into my bedroom." She turned and looked at Chris with an "I told you so," expression. She pointed to her ring finger. Chris looked away.

"Right," Emma nodded. And headed to Nadia's room.

Peter's first stop was in Malba. He pulled up and surveyed the house. This was it, all right, Ricky's place. He headed to the front door but stopped at the mailbox in front, seeing that it read, "Hirschman."

Strange. He hadn't seen that last time. The door opened to a middle-aged man. "Can I help you?"

Peter said, "I hope so. I'm looking for Ricky Grasso?"

"Ricky? I know him, but he doesn't live here."

Peter's brows rose. "This isn't his house?"

The man chuckled. "No! My wife and I have lived here for fifteen years."

"Ricky had a party here for his sister a few weeks ago."

His wife had come to the door and now they looked at each other.

The man's brows creased. "We've been in Israel for a month. Just got back two days ago."

Peter took a deep breath. "You gave him permission to use your home?"

"We certainly did not!" put in Mrs. Hirschman, a short woman sporting a comfortable amount of extra weight.

"How big a party?" asked her husband.

Peter's mind—and heart—were spinning. "I'm sorry, I can't talk now. I have to go!"

"Wait, wait!" Mr. Hirschman called. "We need to know more."

"Ask Ricky," Peter said, already at the door of his car. As he drove off, his mind was doing backflips. Since the night of the party when Ricky hadn't seemed to know how to direct Peter to a restroom, he'd had doubts about the man. He'd even put a tail on Ricky but he'd never bothered to read the report from the private eye. Grasso wasn't important enough. But now he was sorry. This was a game-changer. Something was going on, and he had to find out what it was.

He called Nelson through the car's system. "Remember that guy Ricky Grasso we put the tail on?...I need you to read the report on him. It's on my desk somewhere. I don't want anything mundane or typical. Find what's unusual and give me a call."

Nelson was invaluable—he did everything from valet service to personal research. And he had friends in the FBI and could get intel on practically anyone.

His mind moved to Emma. If Ricky wasn't on the up-and-up, neither was she. But it couldn't be! He was no fool. Sure, he'd not judged Lila correctly, but Emma was different. While he made his way to Nadia's apartment, he called Sy.

"Peter!" Sy always had a hearty greeting voice, even now when it was going on eleven at night.

"How well do you know Ricky Grasso?"

"Huh? Ricky? I knew him when I was teaching. We hadn't been in touch until recently when he called me. He was a decent teacher, a good guy. Why?"

"Did you know that house where he had the party isn't his?"

Sy hesitated. "I thought it was…but I'm not sure he said it was. He just said to come there for the party."

"You've never been to his house before?"

"Um. No, now you mention it."

"Sy, think. Whose idea was it to get me to test Emma? Yours or his?"

Sy fell quiet a moment. "Well, he said he needed a bigger fish to test his girlfriend. So I guess that makes it Ricky's idea, officially."

"Uh-huh," said Peter.

"Why? You think he's up to something?"

"Well, he's a phony. The homeowner was there tonight, and he had no idea Ricky used his place."

"Oy! I can't believe it!"

Nadia Haseltine's building came into view. Peter sighed. "I gotta go."

"Anything else I should know?"

"You and me both," Peter said, thinking there must be a lot more he had yet to discover. "What's your gut feeling about Emma?"

"Good. Sophie loves her."

"Thanks. Gotta go."

"What's this about, boss?"

"I'm not sure yet."

Peter had to circle the block to find a parking spot around the corner. After walking back, he went inside, found Nadia's name and pressed the bell.

When the bell rang, Nadia and Chris stared at each other. "OH. MY. GOSH!" Nadia exclaimed. "It's the mob!"

Chris said, "I don't think so. They wouldn't be after Emma yet."

Nadia nodded. "That's right. So who can it be? I'm not expecting anyone!"

Emma came out of the bedroom. She'd slept fitfully but not very long. "Did I hear the bell?"

Nadia nodded. "We don't know who it is."

Emma's eyes widened. "Oh, no! It's the mob!"

Chris said again, "They wouldn't be looking for you yet."

Emma realized he was right and nodded.

Nadia sat up, exclaiming, "But Peter is! I'm gonna let him in!"

"No!" Emma cried. "Don't you dare! You don't even know it's him!"

"C'mon, Em," her friend said. "You are heartbroken over the guy and he is feeling the same way." She paused. "I'll let him in and then you tell him. Just tell him."

"He'll hate me. That's worse than dying."

"He won't hate you."

"He'll marry you," put in Chris, making Nadia nudge him in the side. "You should talk about marriage!" Wide-eyed, she continued, "What do you know about it?"

"I thought you wanted them to get married!" he exclaimed.

"I do! But be quiet. You'll scare her."

"That doesn't scare me," said Emma. "Telling him the truth scares me. And besides, you don't even know it's him!"

There was a knock at the door and all eyes turned toward it.

"Nadia? It's Peter Bentsen. I know you've got Emma in there." Peter didn't know, but hoped so.

The three in the room froze. Then Nadia jumped to her feet. Emma lunged to stop her but missed. Nadia ran to the door and opened it. She sized up Peter in a second and smiled widely.

"You're Peter."

"I am."

"I'm glad you showed up!"

"Is she here?"

Nadia smiled again. Peter looked around her and saw Emma, large-eyed, sad, vulnerable, standing there. She'd changed into plain sweatpants and a sweatshirt and was barefoot, but she looked every bit as wonderful to him as she had earlier in the red gown.

He rushed past Nadia and took Emma into his arms and held her. She sobbed on his shoulder. Moving apart, he looked at her searchingly. "Why? Why'd you run?"

"It's a long story," she said sadly.

"And I want to hear it. All of it." His brows rose. "But first, I have to do something." He took her hand and sat her down on a chair. Chris began dragging an unwilling Nadia from the room, her eyes fixed on the couple. Peter knelt in front of Emma. He drew her red shoe from his pocket, lifted her foot, and slipped it on. Nadia's eyes grew large before the shoe was on Emma's foot and she broke from Chris's hand and dashed to her room and back. "Here," she said, giving Peter the other red pump.

"Thank you," he said, barely taking his eyes off Emma. He took her second foot, raised it and put the delicate pump on.

"That's better." Gentle warmth emanated from his eyes right into Emma's heart.

"Thank you," she said in a small voice. She was mesmerized by his actions, astonished at his lack of reproach, and afraid that if she raised her voice the magic would shatter. She glanced at Nadia, who mouthed the words, "Tell him! Tell him!"

Emma nodded. "Are you ready to hear my story?"

"More than ready."

Nadia and Chris tiptoed from the room, but Nadia kept looking back with a smile.

"He's not gonna hate her," she said.

"He's not," echoed Chris.

They looked at each other. "It's love!"

When they reached the other room, Nadia said, "I'm so thrilled for Emma." She turned to Chris with a pained expression. "But they're gonna get married. And leave us in the dust."

Chris looked uncomfortable.

"You don't love me, do you?" she asked, miserably.

"Of course I do!" Agonized eyes met hers. "I know what you want. Just trust me, okay? We're getting there."

Nadia's eyes lit. "We are?"

He nodded and took her in his arms. "We're close. Just trust me."

Peter was overjoyed to see Emma. She had run from him as if her life was on the line without a word of explanation. It was an awful thing she'd done. But even after learning about Ricky's deception—which implicated her—he was still overjoyed. He was a fool for love. He hadn't even had the "God talk" with her yet—he had no business falling for her, but if he'd had any doubt of his feelings, they were gone now. Emma's actions were suspicious in light of what Ricky had done by faking the address. But he refused to believe she was up to no good. God had led him to her for a purpose.

She'd said she loved him—he hoped it was true.

Sitting with her on the sofa he said, "Tell me why you ran."

"It's part of the story. You'll understand soon."

He touched her hand. "You're not married, are you?"

She cracked a sad smile. "No. Nothing like that."

"Good. Um. Pregnant?"

"No!"

He nodded and motioned at her. "Go on."

Emma went back to the beginning. It had only been two months since she'd met Ricky Grasso, and only a couple of weeks since her nightmare started, but it felt like years. "When I met Ricky, and we started dating, I thought we were serious." She looked up. "I was falling for him."

Peter's eyes clouded, but he nodded stoically. She hadn't met him, Peter, yet, so this was not threatening. Not much.

Emma continued. "He was very sweet and attentive. But one day he turned into someone completely different. He told me that he'd only dated me to get to me because my father owed his mob boss a hundred thousand dollars, and they expected me to pay it back." She sniffed. "He said if I didn't come up with the 'denaro,' they'd kill me and my brother Adam, and Lila and Loreen!"

Peter's expression showed that he felt the injustice of this. "I thought the mob didn't go after women. That they had their own kind of moral code."

She sniffed. "Apparently, they go after women." She looked him squarely in the eyes. "Ricky broke my heart, besides destroying my world. There was never any semblance of our being a couple after that, except for at that stupid party! By then, I hated the sight of him."

Peter nodded. "I wondered about that. I didn't know you hated him, but I could tell you weren't hot for him."

"You were right. And this is where you came in." She squeezed his hand. "I'm so sorry about this, Peter! I couldn't do it! That's why I ran! I'm in love with you!"

He was thrilled to hear her say it, and he had a good idea by now what it was all about, but he said, "Whoa. Slow down. How did I come in and what couldn't you do?" He wanted to understand exactly.

"Ricky found you through Sy. He gave him a story—which I only found out that night from you and Sophia—that he wanted to test me. Well, that was all a lie!"

Peter nodded. "Okay. So the real purpose for my being there was to fall for you."

"I guess so. Ricky warned me to play hard to get." She made a face and said sardonically, "But you made that really easy."

"I was obnoxious, I know. But do you mean, it was an act, your disinterest? And what you told me in the car yesterday about your standards? Is that part of the act?"

Emma turned injured eyes to him. "No! As I said, you made it really easy to decline your advances because honestly, they were repellant. And this morning I expected you to turn right around and take me back to Flushing. I felt like I was saved from death when you said you were okay with that." She gave him a curious, worried, look. "Why were you okay with that? I would think any man in your position would be a playboy, if anything."

"I'll tell you my story after I hear yours." His expression changed. "But are you telling me that your family's lives were at stake and you still wouldn't have slept with me if I wanted you to?"

She let out a heavy breath. "I know, it's totally stupid, right? But I—well, I—" she hesitated and looked at him tentatively. "I don't like talking about this." She lowered her voice. "I was raped when I was fourteen. To be honest, I'm terrified of having sex. It was so painful! It was one of Loreen's boyfriend's…"

Peter's lips tightened and he squeezed her hands in his. "That sucks. –I—I'm sorry, I don't know what else to say. Some men are evil."

Emma continued, "I know—I know anyone in their right mind would have jumped at the chance to be with you, like when you invited me on your yacht—especially when 'said person' just happens to need a hundred grand—but I, well, I'm emotionally driven to a fault. I just couldn't. Ricky wanted me to get compromised and somehow get you to agree to give me a settlement. Which I found abhorrent to begin with, but he gave me no choice." She turned large eyes to his. "He told me you'd be a crude, egotistical narcissist. I went that night filled with dread about what you'd be like and what I was supposed to accomplish. Then, once I met you—when you started being real—I knew I was dead meat because I could never do it!"

Peter put his head back, thinking. "You need the money so badly; I'm puzzled that you didn't try me."

"After what Lila did to you? I thought you'd hate me if I needed money. That's why I ran. Ricky called me when you went to the house and said I had to get it from you tonight! He said I was out of time. But I couldn't handle you hating me or shutting me out!" She started crying. "I wanted to leave you with good memories of me, not thinking I was another Lila!"

Peter was quiet. He rubbed his temples. "You shut *me* out."

She let out a heavy breath. "I'm sorry! I hated doing it." Her cheeks glistened with tears. "I decided I'd rather face the mob than have you despise me. I'd rather die!"

Peter's eyes were fixed on Emma's. "So let me get this straight. We met so that you could get money out of me, only instead of taking my bait, you rebuffed me, having no idea I'd like that."

She nodded, frowning. "I'm stupid, I know!"

"I don't think you're stupid. But then you continued to see me…to keep the plan going?"

She raised her head. "For one thing, I had to answer to Ricky, but I wanted to keep seeing you. Does that surprise you? Is there one single thing about you to dislike? I kept hoping to figure out another way to repay my debt—."

"Your father's debt."

"Yes. This is what you sensed troubling me. I was determined not to ask you, but I couldn't get loans. I only got approved for ten thousand dollars. When I told Ricky he took it as interest. He said it would buy me some time but I still needed to get the full amount." She paused and swallowed. "I have been walking a tightrope every second since he told me about the debt and the threat to my family." She shook her head. "And I knew it was only a matter of time until you saw the real me—the one needing a hundred grand!" Fresh tears started. "And you'd—you'd peg me as another Lila!"

Peter's expression was grim. "Do Lila and Loreen know about this?"

She shook her head. "I asked Ricky why it was all on me, and he said they'd only caught up with the debt recently. They also thought, for some unfathomable reason, that I'd stand a

better chance at getting the money for them than Lila or
Loreen." She paused. "I wished I could have met you without
having any of this hanging over my head! But they put all the
dirty work on me."

Peter took a deep breath. He shut his eyes.

Emma felt she was going to burst into a million pieces. Her
worst fear was coming true! Peter despised her.

He opened his eyes. "Come here." He patted his lap.

Emma moved onto him, her heart rising like a helium balloon.
Peter put his arms around her. "You are not a Lila. You could
have told me this. You should have told me."

Tears filled her eyes, even as relief and gratitude filled her
heart. She bit her lip and buried her head against his chest. "I
was too afraid to lose you."

He lifted her chin and kissed her softly on the mouth. "I
know. Don't worry—I can help."

Chapter Twenty-One

Still on his lap, Emma blinked back more tears. In a near whisper, she added, "I never wanted to ask you for it."

He stroked her hair as she lay against his shoulder. "I know. It's okay." In the silence following, he added, "I mean it."

"I know—you're wonderful!" Emma dried her eyes. Peter kissed her.

Afterward, she sat up to meet his eyes. "Now tell me your story. There's one thing I need to understand. Why is a great guy who's great-looking AND filthy rich, still single?"

Peter's mouth quirked into a little grin. "Your question's understandable, but let's iron out your situation, first. I promise we'll talk about me later and I'll explain everything.

I've been busy adding to the family fortunes if you want the short answer. But for now, you look exhausted. I think you need some rest."

He went to kiss her, but she said, "Peter, I need to know. I need the long answer. You told me at your parents' house that you don't date a lot, and now you've said you've been busy building an empire, but why don't you care—if I can be blunt—that sex is off the menu?"

He smiled softly. "OK. You want to have this conversation now?"

Emma nodded vehemently. "Yes!" She needed to know whether what Lila said about him being gay was true or not. Despite his kisses and embraces, he was hiding something. Why else would he keep seeing a woman who wouldn't allow hanky-panky? Why else make such a mystery of this?

Nadia burst out of her room with Chris trailing behind, and saw Emma on Peter's lap. "I knew it!" she cried, clapping her hands. She came and gave Emma a kiss on the cheek. "I told you he wouldn't hate you!"

Peter looked at Emma with mock reproval, but then kissed her other cheek. "Of course not." Chris, who loved to eat, cried, "We should celebrate! Let's go out and eat."

Emma said tiredly, "Another time."

Peter said, "Emma's had quite a night."

Nadia chimed in, "Yeah, it's not every night a girl runs like Cinderella and gets found by her prince."

Emma looked with shining eyes at Peter. "That's for sure."

"Can I get you anything? Something to drink?" Nadia asked, bright-eyed.

"I'm good, thanks," Emma said.

"Same here," said Peter. "We're about to get going." With a grin, he added, "Thanks for harboring my runaway princess."

"Thank you both!" Emma echoed.

Nadia beamed. "Glad to help." Chris nodded his agreement.

Peter touched Emma's elbow. "We'll talk in the car."

On the pavement, Emma looked down at her shoes appreciatively. "For thin-heeled pumps, these are truly comfortable. Thanks again."

Peter smiled. "Premium brand. Melania Trump buys these."

Emma's eyes widened. "Wow. I'm glad you found the one I dropped!" She wouldn't guess what they must have cost.

They turned the corner and found the black Lamborghini being admired by a few dubious-looking characters in hoodies. Emma would have turned right around if it hadn't been for Peter, who took her elbow and said, "Don't worry."

He put one hand in his pocket and led Emma to the passenger door. "Show's over, guys!" He opened Emma's door but never took his eyes off the young men. When she was seated, he closed her door and turned to stare down the boys. Maneuvering something inside his pocket, he told them, "Like I said, show's over." They looked at his hand in the pocket. He waited until one said, "C'mon, guys," and they all moved off. Then he joined her in the car.

"Is that a gun in your pocket?" Emma asked in awe.

He shook his head. "I'm licensed to carry but I didn't think of it when I rushed out." He turned to offer a smirk. "After a fleeing princess."

"Sorry!"

He studied her. "It's been a long night. Should I take you home?"

Emma looked troubled. "I thought we were going to talk. I get the feeling you don't want to talk about yourself; like—like you're hiding something."

Startled, Peter said, "Hiding? No, I'm not hiding anything. I've just been waiting for the right time to talk about something that's important to me."

Emma's heart filled with dread. She stared at him. "Are you gay?"

Peter gaped at her. "No!" He let out a rueful chuckle. "Wow. I'm sorry if I did anything to give you that impression."

Emma shut her eyes and exulted. "Thank God!" Opening them again, she asked, "But then what is it? Why doesn't sex matter to you?"

He bit his lip and took her hand. "Whoever said it doesn't matter?" To her silence, for she didn't know what to say, he continued, "I've wanted to have this conversation sooner, believe me, but the time never seemed right. Tonight didn't seem right, either." He looked into her eyes. With careful precision, he said, "I'm a Christian, and I take my faith very seriously. I won't have premarital sex, period, because it displeases God."

Her mouth dropped open just enough so that a few teeth showed. "Wow."

His expression faltered. "Wow, what? Wow, that's great, or, Wow, that's nuts?"

She smiled sheepishly. "Just wow. I've never met anyone who, um, cared about that."

"About pleasing God?"

"Yes."

"Maybe you've never met a real Christian. Lots of people claim to be Christians but when they behave however they feel like and disregard what the Bible teaches about morality, including sexuality, it shows they're just deceiving themselves."

Emma grew thoughtful. "I did meet some Christians once. They were very…" She paused, thinking. "Welcoming. Some were especially sweet, but not all." She looked up suddenly. "Does this mean God is not in favor of sex?"

He laughed out loud. "No! He invented it! But he told us how to engage in it and that is with one partner, in marriage, for life."

She stared in amazement. "So you're still a virgin?"

Peter's brows furrowed. "No. I blew it in my teens, I won't lie to you." Seeing her face, he added quickly, "Just one girl! But more than once. I'm sorry."

She shook her head. "You don't have to apologize to me. If I hadn't been abused, I have no idea what my sex life might have been like. I doubt I'd have had the strength to stay pure for purity's sake."

"Well, what I'm trying to tell you," Peter said, smoothing her hair on one side of her face, "is that I'm not doing that, either. I'm doing it for Jesus' sake. Knowing him makes all the difference in the world."

Emma was intrigued. "You feel like you know him? I mean, really know him?"

Peter nodded, smiling gently. "I do. It's not the same as knowing a person in the flesh. I've had… glimpses of Jesus at times, but He's Spirit." He paused. "But that means I can talk to

Him whenever and wherever I want, and because I am His, that is, I gave my life and heart to Him and trusted Him to forgive my sins, I have access to Him at all times. And I trust Him to give me eternal life when I die, just as He promised."

"He promised that?"

"In His Word, the Bible." Peter's blue eyes shone with conviction. Emma asked, "But what makes you abstain sexually if you know all that? That you'll be forgiven and have eternal life?"

Peter spread out his hands. "It's not blanket forgiveness, like a get out of jail free card." He bit his lip. "See, this is how it works. Once you repent of your sin and ask forgiveness, and that means acknowledging that you need a Savior and that Jesus is that Savior, He forgives you and lives inside you. Your desires change. I'm not saying I don't feel temptation, but my greater desire is to please the Lord, so I abstain. And His presence with me helps me do that."   He paused and shook his head. "It's hard to explain, I guess. Jesus said, "If you love me, obey my commandments.' So I do—the best I can, anyway."

He gave her an earnest look. "You are a temptation, believe me. That's why I can't let us get deep and heavy when I kiss you. It would be too much for me." He paused. "But it's not as hard as it sounds—when you know Jesus, you love him. You want to do what's right."

Emma considered this. "What makes you love him?"

"Great question." He looked into her eyes. "Because He loves me. He's forgiven me for everything. Because he died in order to forgive me. When you think about all he suffered when he didn't have to... for our sake."

"He didn't have to? I thought the Pharisees had him killed. I saw a film about him once and I left it feeling like, 'Poor Jesus. If only he'd had a fair trial!"

Peter shook his head, his eyes full of excitement. "No! No. He could have stopped that trial. He could have called down an army of angels from heaven. But he came purposely to die like that, at that time, on that cross, for us!"

Emma frowned. "I don't get how that helps us."

Peter said, "Look, you know you're a sinner, right? We all know it in our hearts."

Emma nodded. "I sure do."

"Well, I'll use an example from a guy I follow on YouTube, Ray Comfort. Let's say you owed a million-dollar fine and were dragged into court. You don't have the money; you can't pay it."

"I know that feeling all too well," Emma interjected.

"Yes, you do, sorry," he said, lifting her hand to kiss it. "But if someone paid your fine for you, the judge could let you go free. The price is paid. Jesus's death on the cross is like that because it was payment for our sin. Unlike us, he didn't commit a single sin. He was and is God in the flesh, absolutely spotless. But he willingly took our sin upon himself—that's what separated him from the Father on the cross, our sin—and he paid the penalty for it, which is death. But he paid it for us. He hadn't sinned himself, so death could not keep him. That's why he rose from the dead. But since he died with our sin on him, to those who believe, we are now free—he paid our price."

"So you don't have to be good, but you are, because you want to keep him happy."

Peter smirked. "Not exactly. Like I said, it's not blanket forgiveness so we can behave however we want. The Bible warns us that we aren't really 'in Christ,' if we're not following the Lord in an obedient life to the best of our ability. It's not like he's holding a whip over our heads, but he loves us. His ways are best for us, both individually and societally."

Emma nodded. "That makes sense."

"You can know the Lord, too," he said, looking at her earnestly. "The Bible teaches that you must turn to God and ask for forgiveness in Jesus' Name. That's repentance, the only condition for receiving Christ and eternal life. And if you repent, you'll be forgiven so that when you die, you'll live in heaven with the Lord for all eternity."

She looked at him curiously. "Is that what you did? You repented?"

He nodded. "I did. When I was nineteen, after that girl and I broke up. I got serious with the Lord and asked his forgiveness. And I put my trust in Christ."

Emma blinked. "And that's it? That's all you have to do?"

Peter chuckled. "Well, if you're serious about it, that won't be all. Once you realize you have a loving, holy God to answer to, one who wants to bring you to heaven, you'll start reading the Bible and find you can't get enough of it. You'll attend a Bible-believing church to grow in your knowledge of God and meet other Christians. Real Christians want to fellowship with other believers, it's part of our calling. And somewhere along the way, you'll find that the sin you used to be comfortable with, isn't comfortable anymore. Whatever it was, lying, stealing, being selfish—or promiscuous—the Lord will slowly transform you and you'll want to please him."

Emma nodded. "It sounds good. I need forgiveness. And it sounds like getting serious with God will help me be my better self."

"He'll help you be the best version of you that can be. Eventually." He grinned. "It's called 'sanctification,' and it takes a lifetime. Sometimes bad habits or desires drop off people immediately when they surrender their life to Christ. But some are left for us to battle out of the flesh over time as we grow in the faith and with the help of the Holy Spirit."

Emma took a deep breath. "So, how do I start? Do I have to go to church?"

He stifled a smile. "You start with a prayer. But I want you to think about this. You see, I was waiting to have this talk because it's so important. When you turn to Jesus, it's for life, it's the best decision anyone can make—but it's a commitment, and you should count the cost. I'll give you a Bible so you can start reading the gospels. That's the best way to get to know Jesus."

He gave her a kiss on the nose. But her eyes clouded.

"What is it?"

"Speaking of cost, I'm still in that courtroom owing a hundred grand! Or I may end up in heaven much sooner than I'd like!"

He kissed her again. "Don't be silly. Someone is paying your price."

Chapter Twenty-Two

Just as Peter went to start the engine, the car phone buzzed and the dash read, "Nelson." Peter clicked the car audio off and picked up his phone. "I gotta take this," he said to Emma. "I'll just be a minute." All Emma heard during the short call was "Uh-huh," "Really?" "No kidding!" and "Got it, thanks, my man." Peter stashed the cell phone into his jacket pocket. Starting the car he said, "So—to your apartment?"

Emma said, "I left my keys in your guest room. I could ask Mrs. Akbari to let me in..."

"Don't bother Mrs. Akbari. I'd rather you came back with me, anyway."

"I'm glad. Ricky said tonight was my last chance. I'm frightened they might come looking for me at my apartment."

He said, "Well, if they come, you won't be there. But soon, they'll have what they're after."

With large eyes, she cried, "This is still sinking in! I've been worried for so long, it's hard to believe I don't have to worry." She turned to him and said, "Peter. I hope you know that I consider this a loan."

He let out a breath of a laugh. "Don't be silly." He shook his head, biting back any further words that came to mind.

"It has to be a loan, because otherwise—I—I just don't know how to thank you!" She wanted to sink into his arms and lean against him, but the front seats were separated by a wide and busy-looking console.

Peter said, "You can thank me, but you should thank God, too." He glanced her way before turning back to the street. "Can you see how the Lord brought me into your life at just the right time? What Ricky planned for evil, the Lord turned into something good. He's watching out for you."

Emma realized he was right, and that she would have missed it had he not pointed it out. Out loud she said with endearing earnestness, "Thank you, God! Thank you for Peter!"

Peter smiled and looked over at her as if he, too, wished they could embrace. She smiled back at him gratefully. She felt like she'd just been released from prison, from an enormous hand that had seized her throat with an iron grip. Peter was covering the debt!

But her eyes clouded with the thought that "enforcers" might come looking for her even in Old Westbury.

She told Peter her fear at the next stoplight, adding, "I hope your folks have a good security system. My apartment doesn't."

"We do. And there's Nelson."

"Perfect," she said.

"You don't know how perfect. Nelson's a former SEAL."

Emma's brows rose. "Wow."

He turned to her looking thoughtful. "Call Ricky right now and tell him I'll pay up. That ought to keep the wolves at bay for the time being."

Emma pulled her cell phone out. When Ricky picked up, she said, "It's Emma. Peter's agreed to give me the money."

Ricky paused. "Are you trying to put one over on me?"

"No. He promised."

"What'd you tell him?"

She paused. "I said my father owed money and I wanted to pay it back."

Ricky exploded. "Did you tell who he owes it to? Did you tell about my connections?"

"No. I said it was my lifelong ambition to pay back the debt and he said there was no need for that. He would help." Emma looked uncertainly at Peter. Would he think worse of her for lying?

"I don't believe it."

Emma's voice rose. "Because he's not like you. He's a good man!" She glanced at Peter and saw he looked pleased.

Ricky paused. "What does 'he'll help' mean exactly? I need him to pay it all."

"He will. He promised. I have to go."

"Call me tomorrow to arrange the pickup for Monday. It has to be cash." He paused. "And princess… you'd better be telling the truth."

Emma took a shuddering breath and put her phone away. "I hate that man. And I don't trust him."

Peter looked concerned. "He calls you princess too?"

She frowned. "He did when we dated, but now it's a dig."

He blew a kiss toward her. "You're still Princess Emma to me."

She took his hand from the wheel and kissed it, smiling.

Peter turned onto a ramp for the Long Island Expressway. For the rest of the drive, he had her tell him exactly how it had started, what Ricky said when he broke it to her. Emma thought back to that horrible day. She'd been expecting to eat out with Ricky at a new restaurant. Instead, as soon as she got in his car, he turned to her and said, "We're not going out." His large olive eyes stared into hers but in place of their usual warmth was a piercing, cold gaze. "I have something to tell you. Listen. Very. Carefully."

Emma's heart froze, though she had no idea what to expect. He continued, "I am not your boyfriend. I'm a collector."

"A what?"

"I collect debts. For the mob."

Emma's eyes widened. "Okay. But—but you're not my boyfriend?"

"Listen!" he said, sharply. "Your father died owing a great deal of money to very dangerous men."

"My father owed money?" This wasn't too surprising; after he died, they'd found out he was broke. But owing money was another thing. "To who?"

He stared out the front windshield. "I told you. The mob. He owed a hundred grand. And somehow, it's gotta be paid." He turned his gaze back to her. "It's on you, princess, to pay it."

"A hundred grand? My father? He couldn't have!"

Ricky shrugged. "He played horses. And borrowed from the wrong guys."

Emma let out a gasp of disbelief. "He might have owed money, but not that much."

Ricky's hands were on the steering wheel though he hadn't started the car. His grip tightened, the knuckles whitening his tan Italian skin. Blazing eyes bore into hers but his voice, when he spoke, was controlled. "He owed more than that, but he paid off some."

Emma couldn't believe it. Her father had bet at the tracks, that much she knew. And she'd gathered that he lost money. But a hundred grand? It was inconceivable. She swallowed and said, "So this is why we're through? You don't want to see me because my dad died owing money?"

He turned contemptuous eyes to her. "Don't you get it? I needed to get close enough to know if I could work with you on this."

"On what?"

With exaggerated patience, he said, "On getting that money to pay them back. The family would rather get the money than take it out on you and yours."

"The family. Who are they?"

He grimaced. "That's not your concern."

Emma's mind was racing. "How would they take it out on us? Prosecute us?"

Ricky gave a bitter laugh. "Oh, princess, you are clueless. You come up with the money—everything's cool. You don't—your family, including you, are toast."

Emma's throat grew tight. "What do you mean, toast?"

He frowned. "If you don't find a way to pay, you and your family are gonna end up at the bottom of the Hudson. They don't play games."

Emma felt her world crumbling. Her mind spun wildly. "How am I supposed to get that much money?"

"That's something I'm gonna help you with."

Emma thought frantically. "My father died three years ago. Why is this happening now?"

Ricky shook his head. "I don't know. It is."

"I still can't believe he owed that much and wouldn't warn us!" Emma blinked back tears.

"Yeah, yeah, you thought your dad was a saint. Gambling brings out the worst in a man, princess."

"Don't call me that, anymore!"

Ricky shot her a dispassionate glance. For a fleeting second, his eyes softened. "I'm arranging a way for you to get the money. I'll call in a few days and let you know what to do." He leaned toward her.

Emma pounded a fist into his shoulder. "I hate you!" She could not hold back the tears.

Ricky paused. "I'm not your biggest problem. I'm just a collector. If you don't come through, they'll send enforcers. They're the ones to worry about." When she said nothing, just turned away and stared unseeingly out the windshield, he continued, spreading out his hands toward her. "Look. I'm doing you a favor by letting you pay the whole thing. One hundred grand, one payment, and you're free. I could keep you paying the vig for the rest of your life, like your father was. You pay the vig, everyone's happy, but you'd be doing it forever. You'd end up paying way more than a hundred grand."

"What's the vig?"

"Interest. In your case, four thousand a week."

"A week?" She slumped in her seat. "It may as well be a million. I can't pay that."

"That's why I'm in this with you. If you don't come through, it's on my head, too. In the meantime, say nothing to anyone."

"Can I tell Adam?"

"No."

"What about my stepmother and stepsister?"

"Not a word. They hate your father—you told me so yourself—they won't take ownership of this. And they're dumb enough to go to the police. If you fail, maybe they'll try your brother before throwing him overboard with weights—"

"Leave him out of this! He has good memories of my dad. Let him keep them."

Ricky shrugged. "Fine. But remember—if you go to the cops or the FBI, they'll know. They'll go for Adam first, then the others. And then you."

She stared at him tragically, her mind still reeling as her world crumbled. It had been a nightmare ever since. She related the conversation to Peter to the best of her memory.

Peter nodded, listening. Afterward, he asked, "Did he give you any proof that he's telling the truth?"

Emma was stunned. She hadn't thought about this. "What kind of proof would he have?"

Peter said, keeping his eyes on the road, "Something in writing, a promissory note, I don't know." She was silent so he continued, "Did your dad really have a gambling problem?"

Emma sighed. "I didn't see it for what it was. Lila and Loreen knew, but I guess I didn't want to see it. When I was little, he went to Belmont a lot. He took me a few times. Also, to Aqueduct. Later, he mostly stopped going but I guess he was placing bets online. Things got tight, and he gave excuses, which I wanted to believe. I knew he lost money, but I had no idea he was borrowing any."

Peter nodded. "Who are you supposed to deliver the money to?"

"To Ricky, I guess." Emma's brow creased. Could it be that Ricky made it all up?

Peter was quiet. Emma fell silent also, trying to remember any red flags that Ricky's story might be just that—a story. Finally, she said, "What if he made it up?"

Peter said, "It's a good possibility. He is a gambler himself."

"He is? I didn't know that." She was about to ask how he knew it, but he continued, "Did you know that that house in Malba isn't his?"

She gasped. "What? Where he had the party?" She was silent a moment. "I guess I just assumed it was."

"I went there first tonight when I was looking for you."

"You thought I'd be with Ricky?"

He shook his head. "I didn't know what to think. But it seemed like, since you were running from me, it would make sense that you'd run back to him." He shot her an earnest look. "Sorry." He turned back to the road but continued, "Here's the thing. I met the real homeowners, and they had no idea he used their house for a party."

Emma's eyes bulged. She sighed. "I know this must be important, but I'm not sure what it means except Ricky is twice the snake I thought him."

"We'll find out."

"What do we do in the meantime? To put off paying?"

Peter took a deep breath, thinking. "All we need is some time to get to the bottom of it." He was silent a minute, then glanced at her. "We'll pay the vig."

Chapter Twenty-Three

Peter hit a button and the car filled with soothing classical music. "Put your seat back and rest. We'll talk more at the house."

Emma must have dozed off, for it seemed only minutes later that they arrived in front of the estate. Nelson was already at Peter's door. He climbed in, giving her a nod. Peter helped her from the car and held a protective arm about her as they went to the house.

Inside, he turned to her. "I should say goodnight but I'm a bit keyed up." He leaned his head in, touching her forehead with his. "I'm going to have a cup of tea. Want to join me?"

Emma was exhausted, but she couldn't pass this up.

Any time with Peter was a treat. And she was keyed up too. "Sure."

In the kitchen, he motioned her to sit at a counter while he pulled mugs from a cupboard. He opened a tea caddy with flavored teas, and Emma chose Chai decaf. Peter chose Earl Grey. He poured steaming water into their mugs from a tap over the sink.

Emma gaped. "Is that instant boiling water?"

He nodded. "It's always ready. Nice, huh?"

They sat together on a loveseat in a little sitting room off the main area. Emma nestled against him and he put an arm across her shoulders. She said, "I'm sorry you're keyed up because of my mess. I'm sorry for what I put you through tonight."

He squeezed her shoulder. "I'm sorry for your mess."

She murmured, "How do you know Ricky's a gambler?"

He took a sip of tea, then put the cup down. "The night of the party, I had a funny feeling about him."

"I'm not surprised. That snake. He's a complete fake."

Peter cleared his throat. "Well, I had someone look into him."

Emma raised her head to meet his eyes. "Oh!" She frowned. "Is someone looking into me, too?"

He chuckled. "No. I'm not in the habit of getting intel on people. I just had a gut instinct after Ricky seemed confused about the location of a restroom in his own house."

She settled back down. "So, he's a gambler."

"Big time. He's addicted to it. And he's broke."

Emma thought about that, but her eyes were growing heavy. "Did you discover his mob ties?"

Peter shook his head. "We weren't looking for that. I had no idea he had ties.

It does seem surprising, though, that we didn't find them in the process." He paused. "But we do know he's borrowing money, and he was seen giving the ring I bought his sister to a bookie."

Emma bit her lip. "And this didn't make you suspicious of me?"

He smirked. "I paid no attention to the report and only found out tonight from Nelson what it said. When I found out Ricky didn't live in Malba it got me curious, so Nelson scanned the report for me. If I'd looked at it earlier, I'd have saved myself a trip."

Emma sipped her tea and put her head back on his shoulder. Snuggling against him, she said, "I wonder if Ricky is the one who really owes the money!"

"I'm wondering the same thing."

"It makes sense that my dad might owe some, but not a hundred thousand. I just know he wouldn't go in the hole that deep."

Peter's tone was soft. "If he needed money for gambling, he might have."

Emma was so tired she didn't want to move. She murmured, eyes closed, "How can we find out the truth?"

"We can start by confronting Ricky."

"He said they'd kill me and my family if I told anyone." Her voice was low and soft.

"To keep you from talking." Peter stroked her shoulder and she snuggled into him further. He continued, "If it turns out that he's been lying all along, then it's likely his own neck he's trying to save, not yours. But I'll find out." When there was silence, he gave her a gentle nudge. "Okay?"

When there was still silence, he looked down at Emma. Her lovely face, so peaceful in sleep, seemed somehow different.

She was always attractive, but he realized he'd never seen her fully relaxed before. He hadn't been able to put his finger on it, but he'd sensed steady caution and distrust in her. Now he knew they were anxiety-based. Even during their best moments together she'd carried this burden of fear and worry, running like a raging undercurrent through everything she said or did. Thanks to Ricky Grasso.

Peter was determined to get to the bottom of it. If Ricky had involved Emma to save his own skin, Peter wouldn't rest until he got him behind bars. If it was indeed the mob behind it all, he'd make a deal or pay the full fee. Either way, Emma wouldn't have to worry about it again.

He kissed her forehead and settled back, putting his legs on the coffee table.

Sleep was a good idea.

Emma awoke next to Peter on the sofa, saw he was asleep, and headed to her room for a shower. She had no idea when they'd leave for church, but she'd get ready.

When she was still gently combing out her wet hair, Peter texted. They'd leave in an hour, he said, but breakfast was available whenever she wanted it. Suddenly it hit her that she hadn't had coffee yet. She hurried into the outfit she'd brought for the day, quickly put on very light makeup, and found Peter sitting with coffee and a small tablet in the breakfast nook. He looked freshly showered also, with cute damp tendrils of blond hair around his face and forehead. Like her, he wore "office casual," which for him meant black jeans, a button-down shirt opened at the neck, and no tie. He looked great.

He closed the tablet at sight of her and smiled. Emma stopped by his chair to give him a quick good morning kiss on the cheek, but he came to his feet in record time and embraced her. After a good hug, he asked, "Coffee?"

"Definitely."

He poured her a cup from a carafe on the table while she sat down. There was a covered dish before her which she opened to find three fluffy blueberry pancakes with blueberry compote on top and bacon on the side. "Wow."

Peter grinned.

"This is a lot of food," she said.

"It's my favorite Sunday breakfast."

Emma nodded. "That's right. You love pancakes. You got in trouble for using a bad word when you didn't get them for dinner that time."

He chuckled. "Guess I don't change much."

She had lifted her fork with a bite of pancake, but stopped, hovering it in the air. Before she knew what she was saying, she blurted, "I hope you never change. You're perfect just as you are." Blushing crazily, she concentrated on eating and wouldn't look at him.

Peter was silent, making her finally peek up at him. He was looking at her intently.

"I'm sorry!" she cried. "Was that too…intense? I—I didn't mean—"

"Too intense?" He leaned toward her. "I love that you said that. Thank you."

"Oh." Her voice came out low but laced with relief. Their eyes met and held, until Peter waved at her plate. "Please, eat."

Later, after the most interesting church service Emma had ever attended, she went up for the altar call with no hesitation except for feeling self-conscious. When Pastor Hughes asked, she knew that yes, she wanted Jesus Christ to be Lord of her life. And yes, she was willing to repent in order to be forgiven and washed clean of her sins. Finally, yes, she wanted to look forward to an eternity in heaven with the Lord and all his people.

She returned to their pew to a smiling Peter, who kissed her cheek.

Emma had yet to process all that happened, but so far she had a crazy feeling of joy. She even saw everything that had happened with Ricky, all the hurt, worry and fear, had worked out for her good. She'd found salvation in Jesus, and she'd found Peter. Would either have happened if Ricky hadn't entered her life? Not likely.

She didn't know for sure how long she and Peter would be together. She knew she would marry him in a heartbeat, but he hadn't asked. They'd only known each other for a couple weeks, but it felt like she'd known him for ages. In any case, he was a blessing, and she wouldn't worry about the future now.

After talking in the car about the service and Emma's "official" conversion to Christendom, they arrived back at the house where Peter wanted to discuss how to proceed with Ricky.

They weren't hungry yet, so he called Nelson to join them. To Emma's surprise, two more men in suits came with him. Peter introduced them as FBI agents!

Nelson told Peter, "They got my scoop already."

They sat down and had Emma tell her story from the beginning, from when Ricky first approached her at the bus stop in Flushing. She told them how he'd first become her boyfriend but then showed his true colors. She told all that he'd said about her father owing money, all the threats, and how he'd instructed her to try and con Peter into paying up. When they'd heard everything, the men assured Peter that they'd take care of it.

"Wait," Peter said, his brows furrowed. "If the mob is involved, I'm going to pay them. I don't want anything left hanging that could threaten Emma."

One of the men sighed. "Look. We'll figure out if there are ties; but don't pay. That only encourages them."

"I'll only pay interest," Peter said. "Until we find out what's going on."

"That's probably Grasso's plan," the other man said. "He'll keep the bulk of the dough, clear up his own debts, and pay the vig to keep the family happy. That's why he wants it all at once from Emma."

Peter took Emma's hand and squeezed it. He said, "Either way, we're pressing charges against Ricky for extortion and for threatening Emma's life." Emma flushed with pleasure. It felt wonderful to have someone else care so much. "We're" pressing charges, he'd said. They were in it together.

"You can do that," one of the men said. "These guys don't go out on a limb to save someone who's been careless. Ricky'll be on his own."

The men gave Peter contact information and some instructions in case he or Emma had anything new to report. They took Emma's information and asked to see her phone in order to bug it! Peter nodded at her to let them, so she handed it over reluctantly.

About five minutes later, they thanked the men for their time, especially on a Sunday. Nelson escorted them out.

When they'd gone, Peter handed her his phone. "Call Ricky. Ask him where and how to pay."

Emma said, "But didn't they tell you not to?"

He frowned. "It's not their lives on the line."

"But what if Ricky made it all up and he's the only one owing money? I don't want you to pay that snake."

"They've got a tail on him, and they'll know when I pay him. When he uses the money, they'll know whether it's for the mob or just his bookies. Either way, he's gonna end up in prison, and that's all I care about."

Emma's face was sober. "Don't pay more than the interest, okay?"

Chapter Twenty-Four

When Emma called Ricky a few minutes later, he went
into a tirade of warnings. She'd better not have involved the
cops, she'd better be telling the truth, have the full amount,
and so on. Finally, he named a diner on Northern Boulevard
in Flushing for them to meet up and give him the money on
Monday, the following day. Once it was counted and found to
be complete, Emma would never hear from him again.

He wanted to meet at noon, but Peter said he couldn't get
that much cash that early.

Emma was afraid to go home in the meantime, but Peter's
parents were set to return Sunday evening, and even Peter
didn't want to wait for their arrival.   First, he'd take Emma to
stop at home for an overnight bag so she could stay with Nadia.

He'd go into Manhattan and get some work done. Then, he'd take Nelson and meet Ricky the following day. He wouldn't hear of taking Emma along, and she was fine with that.

Before they parted, she moved up to him and put her arms around his neck. "Thank you. You're saving my life."

"Maybe. Maybe we're just saving Ricky's neck."

"Either way, you got me out of it."

"By God's grace." He smiled.

She nodded and kissed him. "Yes. By God's grace." She moved away to look up at him. "You're only paying interest, right? The vig?"

He kissed her again. "Don't worry, I've got it."

By Monday morning, Peter's men discovered that Ricky was in the hole to certain loan sharks to the tune of $80,000. The loan sharks were mob affiliates, but his men had contacts who found out they were only after Ricky for repayment, not Emma or her family.

Emma had never been in danger from the mob.

But with Ricky, it was another story. Every week, he had to pay the vig, which was "two points" or $1600 bucks. If he missed a payment, the amount was added to the loan. His house had been confiscated by one loan shark and used to cover interest payments. Ricky'd been living on that but still racking up more debt. And he was running out of time. The money from the house sale was running out. When it did, he'd be liable for the vig each week. Unless he could pay off the loan.

Peter guessed that Ricky had known Emma's father, probably having met him at the tracks. But why he chose to pursue the man's family using Emma, he wanted to find out.

He made a few choice calls, got $20,000 in cash—the amount owed by Mr. Benson, if he owed any—and met Ricky at the diner. He had a closed suitcase on the table when Ricky arrived. He looked over Peter and frowned, but he saw the suitcase and sat down.

"I told Emma to come, not you."

"I told Emma not to." Peter's eyes held his gaze.

Ricky glanced at the suitcase. "That doesn't look like the full amount."

"It isn't."

Ricky's eyes blazed. "I knew I couldn't trust that—"

"Un-unh," Peter said warningly. "Could she trust you?"

"What does that mean?"

"I know that you're the one in the hole for at least $80,000. But you're trying to extort it all from her."

Ricky's lips hardened. "Look. Her old man owed me money when he died."

"Not the mob."

"No, not the mob, to me." His voice was firm and belligerent.

"They're only after you, not her."

Ricky's face grew red. "All I have to do is tell them that $30,000 of that debt was her dad's."

"$20,000. But he didn't borrow it from them." Peter was as calm as a still pond.

"No, he took it from *me*. And he never even paid the vig." Ricky came short of slamming his fist on the table. "It wasn't fair!

I had to borrow that much more because he didn't come through! He swore he had it. I have to answer for that *denaro!*"

"$80,000 of it, not $100,000."

"With interest, it's even more! I gave Emma a break. The vig on her dad's loan is over $15,000 that I've had to pay."

Peter drew in a lazy breath. "What you did to Emma was unconscionable."

"I needed to scare her, or she would never have cooperated. Her father owes me." Ricky's smooth face was ugly in rage, hardened, his eyes like flint.

Peter said, "I brought her father's payment."

"With interest? $35,000. It's been years. You could pay the whole thing. What's it to you?"

"Show me the contract he signed, agreeing to that."

Ricky raked his hand through his hair. "We had a verbal agreement."

"You don't have proof that you lent him a dime, do you?"

Peter's cool blue eyes bore into his. "You're lucky to get anything today."

"Look, I didn't pick Emma's name out of a hat. Her father, Danny Benson, begged me to loan him cash, and I did. To my everlasting regret. The nice guy finishes last, all right. He died shortly afterward, and I got nada, *niente.*" He paused. "He told me he had a lot of cash coming, an inheritance or something. I thought it was a sure bet."

Peter sat back and sipped his coffee. "Looks like you never place good bets."

Ricky's eyes clouded with anger. "Okay, I was stupid. But he owed me, and all I had was his family. Emma was the best prospect, so I went for her."

"Why'd you wait three years? Her father died three years ago."

Ricky looked away and then back at Peter. "I didn't have a plan. 'Til I heard about Sy's job and who he worked for. It's too bad you broke up with Lila, because Emma's dad borrowed the money for her."

Peter's eyes widened. "For Lila? Not for gambling?"

"For Lila. She got herself into some kind of trouble. I think she stole a necklace from someone. I had just won a bundle, close to fifty grand, and Danny swore he'd have it back to me within the week."

While Peter ingested this fascinating twist, Ricky continued, "Turned out, it was good I went for Emma, because it seems you like her more than her stepsister."

Peter folded his hands on the table. "So let me get this straight. You owe the mob $80,000. Emma's dad owed you $20,000—money he borrowed to saved Lila's neck—and you were hoping I'd pay it all. You'd be off the hook, and 20,000 dollars richer."

"Not exactly. I'd still be taking a $15,000 loss for all the interest I never got."

"As a loan shark."

Ricky waved a hand. "If you like. As a loan shark."

Peter sighed. At that moment, the outside door opened and Emma came rushing in with Nadia and Chris behind her. She saw Peter and made a beeline for him, sitting down beside him and throwing herself into his arms. "Thank God, you're okay!"

Nadia and Chris stopped at the table. Nadia spied Ricky and cried, "So you're the snake!"

"Be quiet," Ricky said, looking at Emma.

Peter drew her arms from around his neck to look into her eyes. "Why did you come?"

Emma glanced at Ricky and drew out her phone. "He texted me this morning—but I didn't see it, somehow. That if I didn't come myself, alone, he'd shoot you! I—I just panicked. I texted you but you didn't answer."

Peter frowned. "Sorry." Turning to Ricky he said, "This isn't the first time you've made a death threat, is it?"

"If I don't pay up, at least the vig, *my* life is on the line! I am under a death threat, see?"

"Sounds like you'd be safer in prison," Peter said.

Ricky shook his head. "I'm not going to prison. I don't owe the feds, I owe the family."

Peter nodded to Nelson and another man who had been sitting at the counter not far off. Turning back to Ricky he said, "You're guilty of extortion, fraud, making death threats, occupying a home unlawfully that wasn't yours…and I'm sure there's more."

Ricky looked startled. He grabbed the suitcase to make a run for it, but Nelson and another man who had been sitting at the counter jumped to their feet to intercept him. They needn't have bothered. Chris stood there with his arms crossed, his huge bulk blocking Ricky from going anywhere.

The guy with Nelson came and put handcuffs on Ricky. "You have the right to remain silent. Anything you say can and will be used against you in a court of law."

Ricky's lips were pressed together as though he wanted to scream. His body shivered as if with uncontrollable anger.

"You have the right to an attorney. If you cannot afford an attorney, one will be provided for you." The undercover officer nodded at Ricky to move.

Emma gazed at Ricky sadly. When he glanced at her, she shook her head. "How could you?" she asked. "How could you?"

Sober-faced, he studied Emma. His eyes softened. "I had no choice, princess. I had no choice."

His use of the term, 'princess,' she sensed, was without the usual dig. But she replied, "There's always a choice."

Peter put his arm around her.

The diner fell silent in their immediate area as everyone gawked at the man being walked off in cuffs. Peter led Emma, followed by Nelson, Nadia and Chris, outside after them.

Emma wanted to cry. She pulled a tissue from her purse and wiped her eyes.

"It's over," Peter said soothingly, squeezing her shoulder.

"You're free!" Nadia added, wistfully.

"What happened?" Emma asked. "You didn't tell me you'd be getting him arrested."

Peter gave her a quick rundown. He added, "As soon as I learned that the mob was never after you, I had no choice but to get him in custody."

Nadia's eyes were saucers. "The mob was never after Emma? Oh. My. Gosh."

Emma laughed through tears.

Chris watched her in concern. "Don't cry. Look. Stop, everyone." The little group came to a stop on the sidewalk of Northern Blvd, busy with cars and pedestrians. Ignoring all that, Chris dug in his pocket. "I was gonna save it for tonight, but—" He turned to Nadia and got on one knee on the sidewalk.

Nadia, wide-eyed, looked like she was holding her breath but ready to burst.

Chris pulled out a little black box and opened it to reveal a sparkling high-set diamond engagement ring. Even Peter's brow rose at the sight of it and he nodded his approval. It was huge, at least a carat.

"I was waiting so I could pay cash for this without touching the house fund," Chris explained with big eyes, looking up at Nadia.

Nadia covered her mouth with one hand. Then she exclaimed in astonishment, "You have a house fund?" She glanced at Emma with a look that said, *'Can-you-believe-this?'* Chris said, "Sure. You can't get married without a house." He took a breath. Looking up at her with puppy dog eyes he said, "Nadia Marie Haseltine, I know it's late, and you've been waiting a long time." He swallowed. "But will you marry me? Please, Naddie?"

Nadia gave a sort of strangled squeal. "Yes, yes, yes! You know I will!" She looked ready to jump into his arms but contained herself while Chris placed the ring on her finger. She stared at the ring but before he could rise, she was on her knees too and threw her arms around him. She looked up beaming and grinning from ear to ear at Emma and Peter.

Emma still had tears in her eyes. Happy ones.

Epilogue

SIX MONTHS LATER

Her wedding gown of white satin and embroidered lace was the first dress Emma bought since meeting Peter that he hadn't picked out himself or seen before she came smilingly toward him at the altar. The floor manager at Bentsen's had assured her it was a new arrival, and that even Peter hadn't laid eyes on it. The dress was a mermaid style, fanning out just above the knee to the floor in pleated arcs, ending with a pointed-lace hem. The shoulders and sleeves were lace only, the decolletage scalloped and flirty, and the back a deep vee.

She'd driven to Bentsen's herself to pick it out and for fittings—after Peter taught her to drive and she got her license. He'd taught her in a Lexus, to her astonishment.

But Peter was a good and patient instructor, which helped minimize her worries. She caught on quickly and without a mishap to the car. Then, when she got her license, he gave her the Lexus!

She took Nadia and Chris for pleasure drives, marveling that she was behind the wheel of a car that cost nearly as much as the amount Ricky had hung over her head for so long. All the drama and anxiety associated with Ricky seemed like a bad dream now, except for the fact that it had brought her to Peter. She thanked God for that.

With Peter's encouragement, she'd given two weeks' notice at work as soon as they were engaged. Having more time to study and do artwork was incredibly freeing. Already she had added to her portfolio of finished works with canvases that littered the flat surfaces of her apartment. She did a watercolor of the Old Westbury estate one weekend and Peter had it framed, a gift for his parents. Their delight was an unexpected pleasure—Emma found something unique she could give to her future in-laws who already had everything.

Nadia and Chris were married in Nadia's mother's church. Emma was the maid of honor, and Peter agreed to be a groomsman, though he wasn't best man. Chris's brother Joe filled that spot. And even though Chris was doing well in insurance, Peter found an opening in one of his corporations, which gave Chris a significant raise. Nadia was overjoyed.

The day of the wedding, Nadia did Emma's hair in an elegant chignon surrounded by a slim pearl band and tucked neatly behind a tiara-topped veil. Pastor Hughes, who would also perform the ceremony, happily accompanied her down the aisle.

He led her to a beaming Peter, whose approving, proud, gaze told her she'd made the right choice for her gown. He took her hand and kissed it.

Nadia was a beautiful Maid of Honor, smiling in her summery lavender dress on the arm of Peter's cousin Malcolm, a heavily bearded, slim man. Malcolm and Peter were good friends since childhood and saw each other less of late only because Malcolm now lived in Belgium. Chris looked squeezed in his formal suit sitting in the second row beside Nadia's mother and then Adam. On Adam's other side were a stoic twosome: Lila and Loreen.

From the moment Lila understood that Emma was aware of the truth, her manner changed. She assured Emma that she'd used the money to pay for her necklace—her stepfather insisted upon it. Emma suspected Lila did not intend to tell Loreen, but now Emma insisted. She must be told. No longer would Emma let her dad take the bad rap for being broke.

Loreen became eager to please and full of endless apologies. A month later when Emma announced her engagement, both of them had a hard time maintaining this better attitude toward her. Emma imagined they were feeling a little green. But she invited them to the wedding and they came.

She was learning to forgive, for one thing; and, although her father wasn't the ogre they made him out to be, he was hardly innocent. He did use a good portion of each paycheck to support his gambling habit, and Loreen's savings had been drained. Emma felt it was only right to make amends. If Loreen was cooperative and showed her accounts since she married Emma's dad, Peter was prepared to be generous. Peter's parents and various cousins, aunts and uncles, sat on the right side of the church, as did Sy and Sofia and other friends and business associates of Peter's.

On the left side behind Adam and her stepfamily sat Mrs. Akbari, Emma's co-workers, two of Emma's cousins, and a few friends from other departments in the hospital. These made up the invitees, but behind them, Peter's church family congregated, eager to see their very popular bachelor tie the knot. They came in smiling droves, many with wedding gifts. Happily, their attendance was anticipated so that a banquet had been arranged for them in the church basement. Peter and Emma planned to mingle there for a few minutes before leaving for pictures and then a more intimate reception at the Rainbow Room. Why there? Peter wanted Emma to forget the incident with Lila. He hoped their reception would replace it with happy associations. And they'd get some great wedding photos out on the observation deck.

His parents had grudgingly agreed to what was in their opinion a small reception but asked that the couple would allow a "little party" after their honeymoon in Europe. Emma didn't mind a little party, until Peter explained that the ballroom in Old Westbury would be circled with tables, each holding up to ten guests. So much for small. She supposed she'd have to get used to such things as Peter's wife. As well as living in Manhattan! Peter had a penthouse and asked if she would live there after the wedding for at least six months before deciding she didn't like it. To Emma, Manhattan had always been a great place to visit, but to live there was another thing. Time would tell.

When Pastor Hughes said, "You may kiss the bride," their lips met in an earnest kiss, and the exuberant crowd—save her stepfamily who only smiled thinly—broke into cheers worthy of a sports arena before they came apart. Holding hands and smiling together at the crowd, Emma thought, fairy tales do come true.

"Come, Mrs. Bentsen," Peter said with relish, beginning to lead her by the hand off the podium. He flashed that boyish grin. "Or should I say, Cinderella?"

They spent their first night in Switzerland in a room with a breathtaking view of the Alps. Not that they gave it a lot of time—there were other things to get to. Emma had gone for therapy sessions with a Christian counselor for months to talk through her fears. Peter had gone with her a few times. And one day—miraculously, it seemed to her—she was suddenly looking forward to their wedding night and all the intimacy it would bring.

She supposed being head over heels in love had a lot to do with it.

Cinderella Cakes

From an 1870 Chocolatier's Recipe Book

(The original recipe follows.)

UPDATED RECIPE

Ingredients:

2 eggs

1 cup sugar

1 and ¼ cups flour

½ cup cold water

Lemon juice, 1 tablespoon

Baking powder, 1 teaspoon

Baking chocolate, 1 oz., grated

½ cup jelly of choice (4 oz.)

(Strawberry or raspberry work well)

Chocolate éclair icing (Soft chocolate icing that dries hard)

Directions:

1. Mix the flour and baking powder and set aside.
2. Separate the eggs and beat the yolks and sugar together until light.
3. Beat the whites until light, then combine with yolks and sugar. Add grated chocolate.
4. Add the lemon juice and water, then the flour mixture and beat for three minutes.
5. Pour batter into two pans, and bake at 350° F. for 16-18 minutes, or until springy to the touch.
6. Let cool 15 minutes. In the meantime, heat the chocolate to a gentle boil.
7. Spread jelly over one sheet of cake. Press the other sheet over it and allow to cool completely.
8. When cold, cut into little squares and/or triangular pieces. Dip each piece into the hot icing and place on a tray to dry.

Cinderella Cakes
1870 Recipe

CINDERELLA CAKES Use two eggs, one cupful of sugar, one cupful and a quarter of flour, one gill of cold water, one tablespoonful of lemon juice, one teaspoonful of baking powder, one ounce of Walter Baker & Co.'s Premium No. 1 Chocolate, half a tumbler of any kind of jelly, and chocolate icing the same as for éclairs. Separate the eggs, and beat the yolks and sugar together until light. Beat the whites until light, and then beat them with yolks and sugar and grated chocolate. Next beat in the lemon juice and water, and finally the flour, in which the baking powder should be mixed. Beat for three minutes, and then pour the batter into two pans, and bake in a moderate oven for about eighteen minutes. When done, spread one sheet of cake with the jelly, and press the other sheet over it; and when cold, cut into little squares and triangular pieces. Stick a wooden toothpick into each of these pieces and dip each one into the hot icing, afterwards removing the toothpick, of course.

Other Books by Linore Rose Burkard

The Regency Trilogy
Christian Historical Romance in the Time of Jane Austen!
Before the Season Ends
The House in Grosvenor Square
The Country House Courtship

Regency Time Travel Romance
Forever, Lately
Coming in 2023 The Sequel: Forever, Lovely

The Pulse Effex Trilogy
(as L.R. Burkard)
Grid-Down Suspense!
Pulse: World Gone Dark
Resilience: Into the Dark
Defiance: Battle the Dark

The Brides of Mayfair Trilogy
Stand-Alone Sweet and Wholesome Historical Romance
Miss Tavistock's Mistake
Miss Fanshawe's Fortune
Miss Wetherham's Wedding

FREE OFFER

A Highly Sensitive Bride
Sign up for Linore's mailing list to be in the know about
new book releases,
special sales, and promotions. When you do, you'll receive
the super short story, "A Highly Sensitive Bride," as her thank
you.
Sign up here:
https://www.LinoreBurkard.com/newsletter